A HIGH WIND IN JAMAICA

Books by Richard Hughes

Novels

THE FOX IN THE ATTIC

IN HAZARD

A HIGH WIND IN JAMAICA

Children's Stories

THE SPIDER'S PALACE

DON'T BLAME ME

Short Stories

A MOMENT OF TIME

Poems

CONFESSIO JUVENIS

Drama

THE SISTER'S TRAGEDY

A COMEDY OF GOOD AND EVIL

THE MAN BORN TO BE HANGED

DANGER

A High

RICHARD HUGHES

Wind in Jamaica

Harper & Row, Publishers, NEW YORK AND EVANSTON

This book was originally published under the title *The Innocent Voyage*.

A NOTE BY BURTON RASCOE

A HIGH WIND IN JAMAICA (*The Innocent Voyage*) is open to many interpretations, because it is that rare flower, that almost freak or sport in literature, an entirely original product of the subconscious mind, given symmetry and coherence, form and content, beauty and actuality by talent of a most unusually high order. The reader will get from this book precisely what he is able to bring to it. Which is true of all the great allegories in literature from Genesis to *Jurgen*.

I have heard the children in A *High Wind in Jamaica* described variously as natural and as abnormal, as charming and as bestial, as just like children in real life and as creatures of a perverted imagination. I have heard the book described as though it were a clinical report in psychopathology and again as though it were a sweet little nursery tale about pirates. Well, perhaps it is all these things and the children are all the things they have been described as being. But I have heard no one who has read the book speak of it except in those terms which indicate an original and provocative work of genius.

It is a topsy-turvy world that Richard Hughes has created—if you do not divest your mind of the literary patterns your reading has given you in the past. The pirates are not bloodthirsty and ferocious; and innocent children, in effect, take them captive and subject them to the most complete loss of liberty—the loss of liberty which, as in life, is brought about by the inner compulsion, in this case the instinctive obligation, to feed and care for the young. Yet everything in this world Richard Hughes has created is logical and natural and lifelike. This is because, I suspect, that more than most of us Richard Hughes has retained a memory of how the mind of a child works. Or perhaps because he still retains, for all his adult sophistication and talent, for all his poetic genius and for all his experience in the world, many of the mental qualities of a child.

That *A High Wind in Jamaica* will take its place among the strange, individual, beautiful and subtle works of the imagination and will permanently remain there I have no doubt whatever. It is one of the books that belong to Time. That is to say, in my opinion it is a classic.

Burton Rascoe

January 18, 1930

A HIGH WIND IN JAMAICA

CHAPTER ONE

One of the fruits of Emancipation in the West Indian islands is the number of ruins, either attached to the
houses that remain or within a stone's throw of them:
ruined slaves' quarters, ruined sugar-grinding houses,
ruined boiling houses; often ruined mansions that were
too expensive to maintain. Earthquake, fire, rain, and
deadlier vegetation did their work quickly.

One scene is very clear in my mind, in Jamaica. There
was a vast stone-built house called Derby Hill (where the
Parkers lived). It had been the centre of a very prosperous plantation. With Emancipation, like many others, that
went *bung*. The sugar buildings fell down. Bush smothered the cane and guinea-grass. The field Negroes left their
cottages in a body, to be somewhere less disturbed by even
the possibility of work. Then the house Negroes' quarters
burnt down, and the three remaining faithful servants occupied the mansion. The two heiresses of all this, The
Misses Parker, grew old; and were by education incapable. And the scene is this. coming to Derby Hill on some
business or other, and wading waist-deep in bushes up to

1

the front door, now lashed permanently open by a rank
plant. The jalousies of the house had been all torn down,
and then supplanted as darkeners, by powerful vines: and
out of this crumbling half-vegetable gloom an old Negress
peered, wrapped in filthy brocade. The two old Miss
Parkers lived in bed, for the Negroes had taken away all
their clothes: they were nearly starved. Drinking-water
was brought, in two cracked Worcester cups and three
cocoanut shells on a silver salver. Presently one of the
heiresses persuaded her tyrants to lend her a print dress,
and came and pottered about in the mess half-heartedly:
tried to wipe the old blood and feathers of slaughtered
chickens from a gilt-and-marble table: tried to talk sensi-
bly: tried to wind an ormolu clock: and then gave it up
and mooned away back to bed. Not long after this, I believe, they were both starved altogether to death. Or, if
that were hardly possible in so prolific a country, perhaps
given ground glass—rumour varied. At any rate, they
died.

That is the sort of scene which makes a deep impression
on the mind; far deeper than the ordinary, less romantic,
everyday thing, which shows the real estate of an island in
the statistical sense. Of course, even in the transition period one only found melodrama like this in rare patches.
More truly typical was Ferndale, for instance, an estate
about fifteen miles away from Derby Hill. Here only the
overseer's house remained: the Big House had altogether
collapsed and been smothered over. It consisted of a
ground floor of stone, given over to goats and the children,
and a first floor of wood, the inhabited part, reached from
outside by a double flight of wooden steps. When the
earthquakes came the upper part only slid about a little,
and could be jacked back into position with big levers.
The roof was of shingles: after very dry weather it leaked

like a sieve, and the first few days of the rainy season
would be spent in a perpetual general-post of beds and
other furniture to escape the drips, until the wood
swelled.

The people who lived there at the time I have in mind
were called Bas-Thornton—not natives of the Island,
"Creoles," but a family from England. Mr. Bas-Thornton
had a business of some kind in St. Anne's, and used to ride
there every day on a mule. He had such long legs that his
stunted mount made him look rather ridiculous: and
being quite as temperamental as a mule himself, a quarrel
between the two was generally worth watching.

Close to the dwelling were the ruined grinding and
boiling houses. These two are never quite cheek by jowl:
the grinding house is set on higher ground, with a water-
wheel to turn the immense iron vertical rollers. From
these the cane juice runs down a wedge-shaped trough
to the boiling house, where a Negro stands and rinses a
little lime wash into it with a grass brush to make it gran-
ulate. Then it is emptied into big copper vats, over fur-
naces burning faggots and *trash*, or squeezed-out cane.
"There a few Negroes stand, skimming the poppling vats
with long-handled copper ladles, while their friends sit
round, eating sugar or chewing trash, in a mist of hot
vapour." What they skim off oozes across the floor with an
admixture of a good deal of filth—insects, even rats, and
whatever sticks to Negroes' feet—into another basin,
thence to be distilled into rum.

This, at any rate, is how it used to be done. I know
nothing of modern methods—nor if there are any, never
having visited the island since 1860, which is a long time
ago now.

But long before that, even, all this was over at Ferndale: the big copper vats were overturned, and up in the

grinding house the three great rollers lay about loose. No water reached it: the stream had gone about its own business elsewhere. The Bas-Thornton children used to crawl into the cut-well through the vent, among dead leaves and the wreck of the wheel. There, one day, they found a wild-cat's nest, with the mother away. The kittens were tiny, and Emily tried to carry them home in her pinafore; but they bit and scratched so fiercely, right through her thin frock, that she was very glad—except for pride—that they all escaped but one. This one, Tom, grew up; though he was never really tamed. Later he begat several litters on an old tame cat they had, Kitty Cranbrook; and the only survivor of this progeny, Tabby, became rather a famous cat in his way. (But Tom soon took to the jungle altogether.) Tabby was faithful, and a good swimmer, which he would do for pleasure, sculling around the bathing-pool behind the children, giving an occasional yowl of excitement. Also, he had mortal sport with snakes: would wait for a rattler or a black-snake like a mere mouse, drop on it from a tree or somewhere and fight it to death. Once he got bitten, and they all wept bitterly, expecting to see a spectacular death-agony; but he just went off into the bush and probably ate something, for he came back in a few days quite cock-a-hoop and as ready to eat snakes as ever.

Red-headed John's room was full of rats: he used to catch them in big gins, and then let them go for Tabby to dispatch. Once the cat was so impatient he seized trap and all and caterwauled off into the night banging it on the stones and sending up showers of sparks. Again he returned in a few days, very sleek and pleased: but John never saw his trap again.

Another plague of his were the bats, which also infested

his room in hundreds. Mr. Bas-Thornton could crack a stockwhip, and used to kill a bat on the wing with it most neatly. But the din this made in that little box of a room at midnight was infernal: earsplitting cracks, and the air already full of the tiny penetrating squeaks of the vermin.

It was a kind of paradise for English children to come to, whatever it might be for their parents: especially at that time, when no one lived in at all a wild way at home. Here, one had to be a little ahead of the times: or decadent, whichever you like to call it. The difference between boys and girls, for instance, had to be left to look after itself. Long hair would have made the evening search for grass-ticks and nits interminable: Emily and Rachel had their hair cut short, and were allowed to do everything the boys did: to climb trees, swim, and trap animals and birds. They even had two pockets in their frocks.

It was round the bathing pool their life centred, more than the house. Every year, when the rains were over, a dam was built across the stream, so that all through the dry season there was quite a large pool to swim in. There were trees all round: enormous fluffed cotton trees, with coffee trees between their paws, and, in contrast to the general shapeless enormousness of the vegetation, delicate log-wood, and gorgeous red and green peppers: amongst them, the pool was almost completely shaded. Emily and John set tree-springs in them—Lame-foot Sam taught them how. Cut a bendy stick, and tie a string to one end. Then sharpen the other, so that it can impale a fruit as bait. Just at the base of this point flatten it a little, and bore a hole through the flat part. Cut a little peg that will just stick in the mouth of this hole. Then make a loop in the end of the string. Bend the stick, as in stringing a bow, till the loop will thread through the little hole, and jam it with the peg, along which the loop should lie spread. Bait the point, and hang it in a tree among the twigs: the bird alights on the peg to peck the fruit, the peg falls out, the loop whips tight round its ankles: then away up out of the water like pink predatory monkeys, and decide by "Eena, deena, dina, do," or some such rigmarole, whether to twist its neck or let it go free—thus the excitement and suspense, both for child and bird, can be prolonged even beyond the moment of capture.

It was only natural that Emily should have great ideas of improving the Negroes. They were, of course, Christians, so there was nothing to be done about their morals: nor were they in need of soup, or knitted things; but they were sadly ignorant. After a good deal of negotiation they consented in the end to let her teach Little Jim to read: but she had no success. Also she had a passion for catching house-lizards without their dropping their tails off, which they do when frightened: it wanted endless patience to get them whole and unalarmed into a match box. Catching green grass-lizards was also very delicate. She would sit and whistle, like Orpheus, till they came out of their crannies and showed their emotion by puffing out their pink throats: then, very gently, she would lasso them with a long blade of grass. Her room was full of these and other pets, some alive, others probably dead. She also had tame fairies; and a familiar, or oracle, the White Mouse with an Elastic Tail, who was always ready to settle any point in question, and whose rule was a rule of iron— especially over Rachel, Edward, and Laura, the little ones (or Liddlies, as they came to be known in the family). To Emily, his interpreter, he allowed of course certain privileges: and with John, who was older than Emily, he quite wisely did not interfere.

He was omnipresent; the fairies were more localized, living in a small hole in the hill guarded by two dagger-plants.

The best fun at the bathing-pool was had with a big forked log. John would sit astride the main stem, and the others pushed him about by the two prongs. The little ones, of course, only splashed about the shallow end: but John and Emily dived. John, that is to say, dived properly, head-foremost: Emily only jumped in feet first, stiff as a rod; but she, on the other hand, would go off higher boughs than he would. Once, when she was eight, Mrs. Thornton had thought she was too big to bathe naked any more. The only bathing-dress she could rig was an old cotton nightgown. Emily jumped in as usual: first the balloons of air tipped her upside down, and then the wet cotton wrapped itself round her head and arms and nearly drowned her. After that, decency was let go hang again: it is hardly being drowned for—at least, it does not at first sight appear to be.

But once a Negro really was drowned in the pool. He had gorged himself full of stolen mangoes and, feeling guilty, thought he might as well cool himself in the forbidden pond as well, and make one repentance cover two crimes. He could not swim, and had only a black child (Little Jim) with him. The cold water and the surfeit brought on an apoplexy: Jim poked at him with a piece of stick a little, and then ran away in a fright. Whether the man died of the apoplexy or the drowning was a point for an inquest; and the doctor, after staying at Ferndale for a week, decided it was from drowning, but that he was full of green mangoes right up to his mouth. The great advantage of this was that no Negro would bathe there again, for fear the dead man's "duppy," or ghost, should catch

him. So if any black even came near while they were
bathing John and Emily would pretend the duppy had
grabbed at them, and off he would go, terribly upset.
Only one of the Negroes at Ferndale had ever actually
seen a duppy, but that was quite enough. They cannot be
mistaken for living people, because their heads are turned
backwards on their shoulders, and they carry a chain:
moreover one must never call them duppies to their faces,
as it gives them power. This poor man forgot, and called
out *"Duppy!"* when he saw it. He got terrible rheumatics.

Lame-foot Sam was the one who told most stories. He
used to sit all day on the stone barbecues where the
pimento was dried, digging maggots out of his toes. This
seemed at first very horrid to the children, but he seemed
quite contented; and when jiggers got under their own
skins, and laid their little bags of eggs there, it was not
absolutely unpleasant. John used to get quite a sort of
thrill from rubbing the place. Sam told them the Anansi
stories: Anansi and the Tiger, and how Anansi looked
after the Crocodile's nursery, and so on. Also he had a little
poem which impressed them very much:

> Quacko Sam
> Him bery fine man:
> Him dance all de dances dat de darkies can:
> Him dance de schottische, him dance de Cod Reel:
> Him dance ebery kind of dance till him foot-bottom peel.

Perhaps that was how old Sam's own affliction first came
about: he was very sociable. He was *said* to have a great
many children.

2

The stream which fed the bathing-hole ran into it down a gully through the bush. It offered an enticing vista for exploring: but somehow the children did not often go up it very far. Every stone on the way had to be overturned, in the hope of finding cray-fish: or if not, John had to take a sporting gun, which he bulleted with spoonfuls of water to shoot humming-birds on the wing—too tiny, frail quarry for any solider projectile. For, only a few yards up, there was a Frangipani tree: a mass of brilliant blossom and no leaves, which was almost hidden in a cloud of humming-birds so vivid as much to outshine the flowers. Writers have often lost their way trying to explain how brilliant a jewel the humming-bird is: it cannot be done.

They build their wee woollen nests on the tips of twigs, where no snake can reach them. They are devoted to their eggs, and will not move though you touch them. But they are so delicate the children never did that: they held their breath and stared and stared—and were out-stared.

Somehow, the celestial vividness of this barrier gener-ally arrested them. It was seldom any of them explored further: only once, I think, on a day when Emily was feeling peculiarly irritated.

It was her own tenth birthday. They had frittered away the whole morning in the glass-like gloom of the bathing hole. Now John sat naked on the bank making a wicker trap. In the shallows the small ones rolled and chuckled. Emily, for coolness, sat up to her chin in water, and hun-dreds of infant fish were tickling with their inquisitive mouths every inch of her body, a sort of expressionless light kissing.

Anyhow, she had lately come to hate being touched—
but this was abominable. At last, when she could stand it
no longer, she clambered out and dressed. Rachel and
Laura were too small for a long walk, and the last thing,
she felt, that she wanted was to have one of the boys with
her: so she stole quietly past John's back, scowling bale-
fully at him for no particular reason. Soon she was out of
sight among the bushes.

She pushed on rather fast up the river bed, not taking
much notice of things, for about three miles. She had
never been so far afield before. Then her attention was
caught by a clearing leading down to the water: and here
was the source of the river. She caught her breath de-
lightedly: it bubbled up clear and cold, through three
distinct springs, under a clump of bamboos, just as a river
should: the greatest possible find, and a private discovery
of her own. She gave instantaneous inward thanks to God
for thinking of such a perfect birthday treat, especially as
things had seemed to be going all wrong; and then began
to ferret in the limestone sources with the whole length of
her arm, among the ferns and cresses.

Hearing a splash, she looked round. Some half-dozen
strange Negro children had come down the clearing to
fetch water, and were staring at her in astonishment.
Emily stared back. In sudden terror they flung down their
calabashes and galloped away up the clearing like hares.
Emily followed them: immediately, but with dignity. The
clearing narrowed to a path, and the path led in a very
short time to a village.

It was all ragged and unkempt, and shrill with voices.
There were small one-storey wattle huts dotted about,
completely overhung by the most enormous trees. There
was no sort of order: they appeared anywhere: there were
no railings, and only one or two of the most terribly

starved mangy cattle to keep in or out. In the middle of all
was an indeterminate quagmire or muddy pond, where a
group of Negroes were splashing with geese and ducks.

Emily stared: they stared back. She made a movement
towards them: they separated at once into the various
huts, and watched her from there. Encouraged by the
comfortable feeling of inspiring fright, she advanced, and
at last found an old creature who would talk: Dis Liberty
Hill, dis Black Man's Town. Old-time niggers, dey go fer
run from de bushas (overseers), go for live here. De pic-
caninnies, dey neber seen buckras (whites) . . . And so on.
It was a refuge, built by runaway slaves, and still inhabited.

And then, that her cup of happiness might be full, some
of the bolder children crept out and respectfully offered
her flowers—really to get a better look at her pallid face.
Her heart bubbled up in her, she swelled with glory: and
taking leave with the greatest condescension, she trod all
the long way home on veritable air, back to her beloved
family, back to a birthday cake wreathed with stepha-
notis, lit with ten candles, and in which it so happened
that the sixpenny piece was invariably found in the
birthday-person's slice.

3

This was, fairly typically, the life of an English family in
Jamaica. Mostly these only stayed a few years. The
Creoles—families who had been in the West Indies for
more than one generation—gradually evolved something
a little more distinctive. They lost some of the traditional
mental mechanism of Europe, and the outlines of a new
one began to appear.

There was one such family the Bas-Thorntons were

acquainted with, who had a ramshackle estate to the
eastward. They invited John and Emily to spend a couple
of days with them, but Mrs. Thornton was in two minds
about letting them go, lest they should learn bad ways.
The children there were a wildish lot, and, in the morning
at least, would often run about barefoot like Negroes,
which is a very important point in a place like Jamaica
where the whites have to keep up appearances. They had
a governess whose blood was possibly not pure, and who
used to beat the children ferociously with a hair-brush.
However, the climate at the Fernandez's place was
healthy, and also Mrs. Thornton thought it good for them
to have some intercourse with other children outside their
own family, however undesirable: and she let them go.

It was the afternoon after that birthday, and a long
buggy-ride. Both fat John and thin Emily were speechless
and solemn with excitement: it was the first visit they had
ever paid. Hour after hour the buggy laboured over the
uneven road. At last the lane to Exeter, the Fernandez's
place, was reached. It was evening, the sun about to do
his rapid tropical setting. He was unusually large and red,
as if he threatened something peculiar. The lane, or drive,
was gorgeous: for the first few hundred yards it was entirely hedged with "seaside grapes," clusters of fruit halfway between a gooseberry and a golden pippin, with here
and there the red berries of coffee trees newly planted
among the burnt stumps in a clearing, but already neglected. Then, a massive stone gateway in a sort of Colonial-
Gothic style. This had to be circumvented: no one had
taken the trouble to heave open the heavy gates for years.
There was no fence, nor ever had been, so the track simply
passed it by.

And beyond the gate an avenue of magnificent cabbage-palms. No tree, not oldest beech nor chestnut, is more spectacular in an avenue: rising a sheer hundred feet with no break in the line before the actual crown of plumes; and palm upon palm, palm upon palm, like a heavenly double row of pillars, leading on interminably, till even the huge house was dwarfed into a sort of ultimate mouse-trap.

As they journeyed on between these palms, the sun went suddenly down: darkness flooded up round them out of the ground, retorted to almost immediately by the moon. Presently, shimmering like a ghost, an old blind white donkey stood in their way. Curses did not move him: the driver had to climb down and push him aside. The air was full of the usual tropic din: mosquitoes humming, cicadas trilling, bull-frogs twanging like guitars. That din goes on all night and all day almost: is more insistent, more memorable than the heat itself, even, or the number of things that bite. In the valley beneath, the fire-flies came to life; as if at a signal passed along, wave after wave of light swept down the gorge. From a neighbouring hill the cockatoos began their serenade, an orchestration of drunk men laughing against iron girders tossed at each other and sawn up with rusty hack-saws: the most awful noise. But Emily and John, so far as they noticed it at all, found it vaguely exhilarating. Through it could presently be distinguished another sound: a Negro praying. They soon came near him: where an orange tree, loaded with golden fruit, gleamed dark and bright in the moonlight, veiled in the pinpoint scintillation of a thousand fireflies sat the old black saint among the branches, talking loudly, drunkenly, and confidentially with God.

Almost unexpectedly they came on the house, and were whisked straight off to bed. Emily omitted to wash, since

there seemed such a hurry, but made up for it by spending an unusually long time over her prayers. She pressed
her eyeballs devoutly with her fingers to make sparks appear, in spite of the slightly sick feeling it always induced,
and then, already sound asleep, clambered, I suppose, into
bed.

The next day the sun rose as he had set: large, round
and red. It was blindingly hot—foreboding. Emily, who
woke early in a strange bed, stood at the window, watching the Negroes release the hens from the chicken houses,
where they were shut up at night for fear of John
Crows. As each bird hopped sleepily out, the black passed
his hand over its stomach to see if it meditated an egg that
day: if so, it was confined again or it would have gone
off and laid in the bush. It was already as hot as an oven.
Another black, with eschatological yells and tail-twistings
and lassoings, was confining a cow in a kind of pillory,
that it might have no opportunity of sitting down while
being milked. The poor brute's hooves were aching with
the heat, its miserable tea-cup of milk fevered in its udder.
Even as she stood at the shady window Emily felt as
sweaty as if she had been running. The ground was fis-
sured with drought.

Margaret Fernandez, whose room Emily was sharing,
slipped out of bed silently and stood beside her, wrinkling
the short nose in her pallid face.

"Good morning," said Emily politely.

"Smells like an earthquake," said Margaret, and
dressed. Emily remembered the awful story about the
governess and the hairbrush: certainly Margaret did not
use one for its ordinary purpose, though she had long
hair, so it must be true.

Margaret was ready long before Emily, and banged out

of the room. Emily followed later, neat and nervous, to find no one. The house was empty. Presently she spied John under a tree, talking to a Negro boy. By his offhand manner Emily guessed he was telling *disproportionate* stories (not *lies*) about the importance of Ferndale, compared with Exeter. She did not call to him, because the house was silent and it was not her place, as guest, to alter anything: so she went out to him. Together they circumnavigated; they found a stable yard, and Negroes preparing ponies, and the Fernandez children, bare-foot even as Rumour had whispered. Emily caught her breath, shocked. Even at that moment a chicken, scuttling across the yard, trod on a scorpion, and tumbled over stark dead as if shot. But it was not so much the danger which upset Emily as the unconventionality.'

"Come on," said Margaret: "it's much too hot to stay about here. We'll go down to Exeter Rocks."

The cavalcade mounted: Emily very conscious of her boots, buttoned respectably halfway up her calf. Somebody had food, and calabashes of water. The ponies evidently knew the way. The sun was still red and large: the sky above cloudless, and like blue glaze poured over white-hot clay: but close to the ground a dirty grey haze hovered. As they followed the lane towards the sea they came to a place where, yesterday, a fair-sized spring had bubbled up by the roadside. Now, it was dry. But even as they passed a kind of gout of water gushed forth: and then it was dry again, although gurgling inwardly to itself. But the cavalcade were hot, far too hot to speak to one another: they sat their ponies as loosely as possible, longing for the sea.

The morning advanced. The heated air grew quite easily hotter, as if from some reserve of enormous blaze on

which it could draw at will. Bullocks only shifted their
stinging feet when they could bear the soil no longer: even
the insects were too languorous to pipe, the basking lizards hid themselves and panted. It was so still you could
have heard the least buzz a mile off. Not a naked fish
would willingly move his tail. The ponies advanced because they must: the children ceased even to muse.

They all very nearly jumped out of their skins: for close
at hand a crane had trumpeted once desperately. Then
the broken silence closed down as flawless as before. They
perspired twice as violently with the stimulus. Their pace
grew slower and slower. It was no faster than a procession
of snails when at last they reached the sea.

Exeter Rocks is a famous place. A bay of the sea, almost
a perfect semi-circle, guarded by the reef: shelving white
sands to span the few feet from the water to the undercut
turf: and then, almost at the mid point, a jutting-out shelf
of rocks right into deep water—fathoms deep. And a narrow fissure in the rocks, leading the water into a small
pool, or miniature lagoon, right inside their bastion. There
it was, safe from sharks or drowning, that the Fernandez
children meant to soak themselves all day, like turtles in
a crawl. The water of the bay was as smooth and im-
movable as basalt, yet clear as the finest gin, albeit the
swell muttered a mile away on the reef. The water within
the pool itself could not reasonably be smoother. No sea
breeze thought of stirring. No bird trespassed on the inert
air.

For a while they had not energy to get into the water,
but lay on their faces, looking down, down, down, at the
sea-fans and sea-feathers, the scarlet-plumed barnacles
and corals, the black and yellow schoolmistress-fish, the
rainbow-fish—all that forest of ideal Christmas trees

which is a tropical sea-bottom. Then they stood up, giddy and seeing black, and in a trice were floating suspended in water like drowned ones, only their noses above the surface, under the shadow of a rocky ledge.

An hour or so after noon they clustered together, puffy from the warm water, in the insufficient shade of a Panama fern; ate such of the food they had brought as they had appetite for, and drank all the water, wishing for more. Then a very odd thing happened: for even as they sat there they heard the most peculiar sound: a strange, rushing sound that passed overhead like a gale of wind— but not a breath of breeze stirred, *that* was the odd thing; followed by a sharp hissing and hurtling, like a flight of rockets, or gigantic swans—very distant rocs, perhaps— on the wing. They all looked up: but there was nothing at all. The sky was empty and lucid. Long before they were back in the water again all was still. Except that after a while John noticed a sort of tapping, as if someone were gently knocking the outside of a bath they were in. But the bath they were in had no outside, it was solid world. It was funny.

By sunset they were so weak from long immersion they could barely stand up, and as salted as bacon: but, with some common impulse, just before the sun went down they all left the rocks and went and stood by their clothes, where the ponies were tethered, under some palms. As he sank the sun grew even larger and instead of red was now a sodden purple. Down he went, behind the western horn of the bay, which immediately blackened till its waterline disappeared, and substance and reflection seemed one sharp symmetrical pattern.

Not a breath of breeze even yet ruffled the water; but momentarily it trembled of its own accord, shattering the

reflections, then was glassy again. On that the children
held their breath, waiting for it to happen.

A school of fish, terrified by some purely submarine
event, thrust their heads right out of the water, squatter-
ing across the bay in an arrowy rush, dashing up sparkling
ripples with the tiny heave of their shoulders: yet after
each disturbance all was soon like hardest, dark, thick
glass.

Once things vibrated slightly, like a chair in a concert-
room: and again there was that mysterious winging,
though there was nothing visible beneath the swollen,
iridescent stars.

Then it came. The water of the bay began to ebb away,
as if someone had pulled up the plug: a foot or so of sand
and coral gleamed for a moment new to the air: then back
the sea rushed in miniature rollers which splashed right
up to the foot of the palms. Mouthfuls of turf were torn
away, and on the far side of the bay a small piece of cliff
tumbled into the water: sand and twigs showered down,
dew fell from the trees like diamonds: birds and beasts,
their tongues at last loosed, screamed and bellowed: the
ponies, thought quite unalarmed, lifted up their heads
and yelled.

That was all: a few moments. Then silence, with a
rapid countermarch, recovered all his rebellious kingdom.
Stillness again. The trees moved as little as the pillars of a
ruin, each leaf laid sleekly in place. The bubbling foam
subsided: the reflections of the stars came out among it as
if there could never have been a disturbance, however
slight. The naked children too continued to stand motion-
less beside the quiet ponies, shine on their infantile round
paunches.

But as for Emily, it was too much. The earthquake

went completely to her head. She began to dance, hopping laboriously from one foot onto another. John caught
the infection. He turned head over heels on the damp
sand, over and over in an elliptical course till before he
knew it he was in the water, and so giddy as hardly to be
able to tell up from down.

At that, Emily knew what it was she wanted to do. She
scrambled onto a pony and galloped him up and down the
beach, trying to bark like a dog. The Fernandez children
stared, solemn but not disapproving. John, shaping a
course for Cuba, was swimming as if sharks were paring
his toe-nails. Emily rode her pony into the sea, and beat
and beat him till he swam: and so she followed John
towards the reef, yapping herself hoarse.

It must have been fully a hundred yards before they
were spent. Then they turned for the shore, John holding
on to Emily's leg, puffing and gasping, both a little over-
done, their emotion run down. Presently John gasped:

"You shouldn't ride on your bare skin, you'll catch
ringworm."

"I don't care if I do," said Emily.

"You would if you did," said John.

"I don't care!" chanted Emily.

It seemed a long way to the shore. When they reached
it the others had dressed and were preparing to start.
Soon the whole party were on their way home in the dark.
Presently Margaret said:

"So that's that."

No one answered.

"I could smell it was an earthquake coming when I got
up. Didn't I say so, Emily?"

"You and your smells!" said Jimmie Fernandez. "You're
always smelling things!"

"She's awfully good at smells," said the youngest, Harry, proudly to John. "She can sort out people's dirty clothes for the wash by smell: who they belong to."

"She can't really," said Jimmie: "She fakes it. As if everyone smelt different!"

"I can!"

"Dogs can, anyway," said John.

Emily said nothing. Of course people smelt different: it didn't need arguing. She could always tell her own towel from John's, for instance, or even knew if one of the others had used it. But it just showed what sort of people Creoles were, to *talk* about Smell, in that open way.

"Well, anyhow I said there was going to be an earthquake and there was one," said Margaret.

That was what Emily was waiting for! So it really had been an earthquake (she had not liked to ask, it seemed so ignorant: but now Margaret had said in so many words that it was one).

If ever she went back to England, she could now say to people, "*I have been in an earthquake.*"

With that certainty, her soused excitement began to revive. For there was nothing, no adventure from the hands of God or Man, to equal it. Realise that if she had suddenly found she could fly it would not have seemed more miraculous to her. Heaven had played its last, most terrible card; and small Emily had survived, where even grown men (such as Korah, Dathan, and Abiram) had succumbed.

Life seemed suddenly a little empty: for never again could there happen to her anything so dangerous, so sublime.

Meanwhile, Margaret and Jimmie were still arguing:

"Well, there's one thing, there'll be plenty of eggs tomorrow," said Jimmie. "There's nothing like an earth-quake for making them lay."

How funny Creoles were! They didn't seem to realise the difference it made to a person's whole after-life to have been in an Earthquake.

When they got home, Martha, the black housemaid, had hard things to say about the sublime cataclysm. She had dusted the drawing-room china only the day before: and now everything was covered again in a fine penetrating film of dust.

4

The next morning, Sunday, they went home. Emily was still so saturated in earthquake as to be dumb. She ate earthquake and slept earthquake: her fingers and legs were earthquake. With John, it was ponies. The earthquake had been fun: but it was the ponies that mattered. But at present it did not worry Emily that she was alone in her sense of proportion. She was too completely possessed to be able to see anything, or realise that anyone else pretended to even a self-delusive fiction of existence.

Their mother met them at the door. She bubbled questions: John chattered ponies, but Emily was still tongue-tied. She was, in her mind, like a child who has eaten too much even to be able to be sick.

Mrs. Thornton got a little worried about her at times. This sort of life was very peaceful, and might be excellent for nervy children like John: but a child like Emily, thought Mrs. Thornton, who is far from nervy, really needs some sort of stimulus and excitement, or there is a danger of her mind going to sleep altogether for ever. This life was too vegetable. Consequently Mrs. Thornton al-

ways spoke to Emily in her brightest manner, as if everything was of the greatest possible interest. She had hoped,
too, the visit to Exeter might liven her up; but she had
come back as silent and expressionless as ever. It had evidently made no impression on her at all.

John marshalled the small ones in the cellar, and round
and round they marched, wooden swords at the slope,
singing "Onward, Christian Soldiers." Emily did not join
them. What did it now matter, that earlier woe, that being
a girl she could never when grown up become a real soldier with a real sword? She had been in an Earthquake!

But even the others did not keep it up very long.
(Sometimes they would go on for three or four hours.)
For, whatever it might have done for Emily's soul, the
earthquake had done little to clear the air. It was as hot as
ever. In the animal world there seemed some strange
commotion, as if they had wind of something. The usual
lizards and mosquitoes were still absent: but in their
place the earth's most horrid progeny, creatures of darkness, sought the open: land-crabs wandered about aimlessly, angrily twiddling their claws: and the ground
seemed almost alive with red ants and cockroaches. Up on
the roof the pigeons were gathered, talking to each other
fearfully.

The cellar (or, rather, ground floor), where they were
playing, had no communication with the wooden structure above, but had an opening of its own under the twin
flight of steps leading to the front door; and there the
children presently gathered in the shadow. Out in the
compound lay one of Mr. Thornton's best handkerchiefs.
He must have dropped it that morning. But none of them
felt the energy to go and retrieve it, out into the sun.
Then, as they stood there, they saw Lame-foot Sam come

limping across the yard. Seeing the prize, he was about to carry it off. Suddenly he remembered it was Sunday. He dropped it like a hot brick, and began to cover it with sand, exactly where he had found it.

"Please God, I thieve you tomorrow," he explained hopefully: "Please God, you still there?"

A low mutter of thunder seemed to offer grudging assent.

"Thank you, Lord," said Sam, bowing to a low bank of cloud. He hobbled off: but then, not too sure perhaps that Heaven would keep Its promise, changed his mind: snatched up the handkerchief and made off for his cottage. The thunder muttered louder and more angrily: but Sam ignored the warning.

It was the custom that, whenever Mr. Thornton had been to St. Anne's, John and Emily should run out to meet him, and ride back with him, one perched on each of his stirrups.

That Sunday evening they ran out as soon as they saw him coming, in spite of the thunderstorm that by now was clattering over their very heads—and not only over their heads, either, for in the tropics a thunderstorm is not a remote affair up in the sky, as it is in England, but is all round you: lightning plays ducks and drakes across the water, bounds from tree to tree, bounces about the ground, while the thunder seems to proceed from violent explosions in your own very core.

"Go back! Go back, you damned little fools!" he yelled furiously: "Get into the house!"

They stopped, aghast: and then began to realise that after all it was a storm of more than ordinary violence. They discovered that they were drenched to the skin— must have been the moment they left the house. The lightning kept up a continuous blaze: it was playing about their father's very stirrup-irons; and all of a sudden they realised that he was afraid. They fled to the house, shocked to the heart: and he was in the house almost as soon as they were. Mrs. Thornton rushed out:

"My dear, I'm so glad . . ."

"I've never seen such a storm! Why on earth did you let the children come out?"

"I never dreamt they would be so silly! And all the time I was thinking—but thank heaven you're back!"

"I think the worst is over now."

Perhaps it was; but all through supper the lightning shone almost without flickering. And John and Emily could hardly eat: the memory of that momentary look on their father's face haunted them.

It was an unpleasant meal altogether. Mrs. Thornton had prepared for her husband his "favourite dish"; than which no action could more annoy a man of whim. In the middle of it all in burst Sam, ceremony dropped: he flung the handkerchief angrily on the table and stumped out.

"What on earth . . . ?" began Mr. Thornton.

But John and Emily knew; and thoroughly agreed with Sam as to the cause of the storm. Stealing was bad enough anyway: but on a Sunday!

Meanwhile, the lightning kept up its play. The thunder made talking arduous, but no one was anyhow in a mood to chatter. Only thunder was heard, and the hammering of the rain. But suddenly, close under the windows, there burst out the most appalling inhuman shriek of terror.

"Tabby!" cried John, and they all rushed to the window.

But Tabby had already flashed into the house: and behind him was a whole club of wild cats in hot pursuit.

John momentarily opened the dining-room door and puss slipped in, dishevelled and panting. Not even then did the brutes desist: what insane fury led these jungle creatures to pursue him into the very house is unimaginable; but there they were, in the passage, caterwauling in concert: and as if at their incantation the thunder awoke anew, and the lightning nullified the meagre table lamp. It was such a din as you could not speak through. Tabby, his fur on end, pranced up and down the room, his eyes blazing, talking and sometimes exclaiming in a tone of voice the children had never heard him use before, and which made their blood run cold. He seemed like one inspired in the presence of Death, he had gone utterly Delphic: and without in the passage Hell's pandemonium reigned terrifically.

The check could be only a short one. Outside the dining-room door stood the big filter, and above the door the fanlight was long since broken. Something black and yelling flashed through the fanlight, landing clean in the middle of the supper table, scattering the forks and spoons and upsetting the lamp. And another and another—but already Tabby was through the window and streaking again for the bush. The whole dozen of those wild cats leapt one after the other from the top of the filter clean through the fanlight on to the supper table, and away from there only too hot in his tracks. In a moment the whole devil-hunt and its hopeless quarry had vanished into the night.

"Oh Tabby, my darling Tabby!" wailed John; while Emily rushed again to the window.

They were gone. The lightning behind the creepers in the jungle lit them up like giant cobwebs; but of Tabby and his pursuers there was nothing to be seen.

John burst into tears, the first time for several years, and flung himself on his mother; Emily stood transfixed at the window, her eyes glued in horror on what she could not, in fact, see, and all of a sudden was sick.

"God, what an evening!" groaned Mr. Bas-Thornton, groping in the darkness for what might be left of their supper.

Shortly after that Sam's hut burst into flames. They saw, from the dining-room, the old Negro stagger dramatically out into the darkness. He was throwing stones at the sky. In a lull they heard him cry: "I gib it back, didn't I? I gib de nasty t'ing back?"

Then there was another blinding flash, and Sam fell where he stood. Mr. Thornton pulled the children roughly back and said something like, "I'll go and see. Keep them from the window."

Then he closed and barred the shutters, and was gone.

John and the little ones kept up a continuous sobbing. Emily wished someone would light a lamp, she wanted to read: it might help her not to think about poor Tabby.

I suppose the wind must have begun to rise some while before this, but now, by the time Mr. Thornton had managed to carry old Sam's body into the house, it was more than a gale. The old man, stiff in the joints as he might have been in life, had gone as limp as a worm. Emily and John slipped unbeknownst into the passage, and were thrilled beyond measure at the way he dangled: they could hardly tear themselves away and be back in the dining-room before they should be discovered.

There Mrs. Thornton sat heroically in a chair, her brood all grouped round her, saying the psalms, and the poems of Sir Walter Scott, over by heart. Emily tried to keep her mind off Tabby by going over in her head all the details of her Earthquake. At times the din, the rocketing of the thunder and torrential shriek of the wind, which up to now she had hardly noticed, became so loud as almost to impinge on her inner world: she wished this wretched thunderstorm would hurry up and get over. First, she held an actual performance of the earthquake, went over it direct, as if it was again happening. Then she put it into Oratio Recta, told it as a story, beginning with that magic phrase "Once I was in an Earthquake." But before long the dramatic element reappeared—this time, the awed comments of her imaginary English audience. When that was done, she put it into the Historical—a Voice, declaring that a girl called Emily was once in an Earthquake. And so on, right through the whole thing a third time.

The horrid fate of poor Tabby appeared suddenly before her eyes, caught her unawares: and she was all but sick again. Even her Earthquake had failed her. Caught by the incubus, her mind struggled frantically to clutch at even the outside world, as an only remaining straw. She tried to fix her interest on every least detail of the scene around her—to count the slats in the shutters, any least detail that was *outward*. So it was that for the first time she really began to notice the weather.

The wind by now was more than redoubled. The shutters were bulging as if tired elephants were leaning against them, and Father was trying to tie the fastening with that handkerchief. But to push against this wind was like pushing against rock. The handkerchief, shutters, everything burst: the rain poured in like the sea into a sinking ship, the wind occupied the room, snatching pictures from the wall, sweeping the table bare. Through the gaping frames the lightning-lit scene without was visible. The creepers, which before had looked like cobwebs, now

streamed up into the sky like new-combed hair. Bushes
were lying flat, laid back on the ground as close as a rabbit
lays back his ears. Branches were leaping about loose in
the sky. The Negro huts were clean gone, and the Negroes
crawling on their stomachs across the compound to gain
the shelter of the house. The bouncing rain seemed to
cover the ground with a white smoke, a sort of sea in
which the blacks wallowed like porpoises. One small boy
began to roll away: his mother, forgetting caution, rose to
her feet: and immediately the fat old beldam was blown
clean away, bowling along across fields and hedgerows
like someone in a funny fairy story, till she fetched up
against a wall and was pinned there, unable to move. But
the others managed to reach the house, and soon could be
heard in the cellar underneath.

Moreover the very floor began to ripple, as a loose carpet
will ripple on a gusty day: in opening the cellar door the
blacks had let the wind in, and now for some time they
could not shut it again. The wind, to push against, was
more like a solid block than a current of air.

Mr. Thornton went round the house—to see what could
be done, he said. He soon realised that the next thing to
go would be the roof. So he returned to the Niobe-group
in the dining-room. Mrs. Thornton was half way through
The Lady of the Lake, the smaller children listening with
rapt attention. Exasperated, he told them that they would
probably not be alive in half an hour. No one seemed
particularly interested in his news: Mrs. Thornton continued her recitation with faultless memory.

After another couple of cantos the threatened roof went.
Fortunately, the wind taking it from inside, most of it was
blown clear of the house: but one of the couples collapsed
skew-eyed, and was hung up on what was left of the

dining-room door—within an ace of hitting John. Emily, to her intense resentment, suddenly felt cold. All at once, she found she had had enough of the storm: it had become intolerable, instead of a welcome distraction.

Mr. Thornton began to look for something to break through the floor with. If only he could make a hole in it, he might get his wife and children down into the cellar. Fortunately he did not have to look far: one arm of the fallen couple had already done the work for him. Laura, Rachel, Emily, Edward and John, Mrs. Thornton, and finally Mr. Thornton himself, were passed down into the darkness already thronged with Negroes and goats.

With great good sense, Mr. Thornton brought with him from the room above a couple of decanters of Madeira, and everyone had a swig, from Laura to the oldest Negro. All the children made the most of this unholy chance, but somehow to Emily the bottle got passed twice, and each time she took a good pull. It was enough, at their age; and while what was left of the house was blown away over their heads, through the lull and the ensuing aerial return match, John, Emily, Edward, Rachel, and Laura, blind drunk, slept in a heap on the cellar floor: a sleep which the appalling fate of Tabby, torn to pieces by those fiends almost under their very eyes, dominated with the easy empire of nightmare.

CHAPTER TWO

All night the water poured through the house floor onto the people sheltering below: but (perhaps owing to the Madeira) it did them no harm. Shortly after the second bout of blowing, however, the rain stopped: and when dawn came Mr. Thornton crept out to assess the damage.

The country was quite unrecognisable, as if it had been swept by a spate. You could hardly tell, geograpically speaking, where you were. It is vegetation which gives the character to a tropic landscape, not the shape of the ground: and all the vegetation, for miles, was now pulp. The ground itself had been ploughed up by instantaneous rivers, biting deep into the red earth. The only living thing in sight was a cow: and she had lost both her horns.

The wooden part of the house was nearly all gone. After they had succeeded in reaching shelter, one wall after another had blown down. The furniture was splintered into matchwood. Even the heavy mahogany dining-table, which they loved and had always kept with its legs in little glass baths of oil to defeat the ants, was spirited right away. There were some fragments which might be part of it, or they might not: you could not tell.

Mr. Thornton returned to the cellar and helped his wife out: she was so cramped as hardly to be able to move. They knelt down together and thanked God for not having treated them any worse. Then they stood up and stared about them rather stupidly. It seemed not credible that all this had been done by a current of air. Mr. Thornton patted the atmosphere with his hand. When still, it was so soft, so rare: how could one believe that Motion, itself something impalpable, had lent it a hardness, that this gentle, hind-like Meteor should have last night seized Fat Betsy with the rapacity of a tiger and the lift of a roc, and flung her, as he had seen her flung, across two fair-sized fields?

Mrs. Thornton understood his gesture.

"Remember who is its Prince," she said.

The stable was damaged, though not completely destroyed: and Mr. Thornton's mule was so much hurt he had to tell a Negro to cut its throat. The buggy was smashed beyond repair. The only building undamaged was a stone chamber which had been the hospital of the old sugar-estate: so they woke the children, who were feeling ill and beyond words unhappy, and moved into this—where the Negroes, with an unexpected energy and kindliness, did everything they could to make them comfortable. It was paved and unlighted, but solid.

The children were bilious for a few days, and inclined to dislike each other, but they accepted the change in their lives practically without noticing it. It is a fact that it takes experience before one can realise what is a catastrophe and what is not. Children have little faculty of distinguishing between disaster and the ordinary course of their lives. If Emily had known this was a Hurricane, she would doubtless have been far more impressed, for the word was full of romantic terrors. But it never entered her head: and a thunderstorm, however severe, is after all a commonplace affair. The mere fact that it had done incalculable damage, while the earthquake had done none at all, gave it no right whatever to rival the latter in the hierarchy of cataclysms: an Earthquake is a thing apart. If she was silent, and inclined to brood over some inward terror, it was not the hurricane she was thinking of, it was the death of Tabby. That, at times, seemed a horror beyond all bearing. It was her first intimate contact with death—and a death of violence, too. The death of old Sam had no such effect: there is after all a vast difference between a Negro and a favorite cat.

There was something enjoyable, too, in camping in the hospital: a sort of everlasting picnic in which their parents for once were taking part. Indeed it led them to begin for the first time to regard their parents as rational human beings, with understandable tastes—such as sitting on the floor to eat one's dinner.

It would have surprised Mrs. Thornton very much to have been told that hitherto she had meant practically nothing to her children. She took a keen interest in psychology (the Art Bablative, Southey calls it). She was full of theories about their upbringing which she had not time to put into effect; but nevertheless she thought she had a deep understanding of their temperaments and was the centre of their passionate devotion. Actually, she was congenitally incapable of telling one end of a child from the other. She was a dumpy little woman—Cornish, I believe. When she was herself a baby she was so small they carried her about on a cushion for fear a clumsy human arm might damage her. She could read when she was two and a half. Her reading was always serious. Nor had she been backward in the humaner studies: her mistresses spoke of her Deportment as something rarely seen outside the older Royal Houses; in spite of a figure like a bolster, she could step into a coach like an angel getting onto a cloud. She was very quick-tempered.

Mr. Bas-Thornton also had every accomplishment, except two: that of primo-geniture, and that of making a living. Either would have provided for them.

If it would have surprised the mother, it would undoubtedly have surprised the children also to be told how little their parents meant to them. Children seldom have any power of quantitative self-analysis: whatever the facts, they believe as an article of faith that they love Father and Mother first and equally. Actually, the Thornton children had loved Tabby first and foremost in all the world, some of each other second, and hardly noticed their mother's existence more than once a week. Their father they loved a little more: partly owing to the ceremony of riding home on his stirrups.

Jamaica remained, and blossomed anew, its womb being inexhaustible. Mr. and Mrs. Thornton remained, and with patience and tears tried to reconstruct things, in so far as they could be reconstructed. But the danger which their beloved little ones had been through was not a thing to risk again. Heaven had warned them. The children must go.

Nor was the only danger physical:

"That awful night!" said Mrs. Thornton, once, when discussing their plan of sending them home to school: "Oh my dear, what the poor little things must have suffered! Think how much more acute Fear is to a child! And they were so brave, so English."

"I don't believe they realised it." (He only said that to be contradictious: he could hardly expect it to be taken seriously.)

"You know, I am terribly afraid what permanent, *inward* effect a shock like that may have on them. Have you noticed they never so much as mention it? In England they would at least be safe from dangers of that sort."

Meanwhile, the children, accepting the new life as a matter of course, were thoroughly enjoying it. Most children, on a railway journey, prefer to change at as many stations as possible.

The rebuilding of Ferndale, too, was a matter of absorbing interest. For there is one advantage to these match-box houses—easy gone, easy come: and once begun the work proceeded apace. Mr. Thornton himself led the building gang, employing no end of mechanical devices of his own devising, and it was not long before the day came when he stood with his handsome head emerging through the fast dwindling hole in the new roof, shouting directions to the two black carpenters, who, lying spread-eagle in their check shirts, pinned on shingle after shingle—walling him in, like the victim in some horrid story. At last he had to draw in his head, and where it had been the last few shingles were clapt into place.

An hour later the children had looked their last on Ferndale.

When they had been told they were to go to England, they had received it as an isolated fact: thrilling in itself, but without any particular causation—for it could hardly be due to the death of the cat, and nothing else of importance had occurred lately.

The first stage of their journey was by land, to Montego Bay: and the notable thing about it was that the borrowed wagonette was drawn not by a pair of horses or a pair of mules, but by one horse and one mule. Whenever the horse wanted to go fast the mule fell asleep in the shafts: and if the driver woke it up it set off at a gallop, which angered the horse. Their progress would have been slow anyhow, as all the roads were washed away.

John was the only one who could remember England. What he remembered was sitting at the top of a flight of stairs, which was fenced off from him by a little gate, playing with a red toy milk-cart: and he knew, without having to look, that in the room on the left Baby Emily was lying in her cot. Emily *said* she could remember something which sounded like a Prospect of the Backs of some Brick Houses at Richmond: but she might have invented it. The others had been born on the island—Edward, only just.

They all had nevertheless most elaborate ideas about England, built up out of what their parents had told them, and from the books and old magazines they sometimes looked at. Needless to say it was a very Atlantis, a land at the back of the North Wind: and going there was about as exciting as it would be to die and go to Heaven.

John told them all about the top of the stairs for the hundredth time as they drove along; the others listening attentively (as the believing do to a man remembering his reincarnations).

Suddenly Emily recalled sitting at a window and seeing a big bird with a beautiful tail. At the same time there had been a horrid screeching going on, or perhaps something else disagreeable—she could not quite remember which sense was offended. It did not occur to her that it was this selfsame bird which had screeched: and anyhow it was all too vague for her to try and describe it. She switched off to wondering how it was possible actually to *sleep* when walking, as the driver said the mule did.

They put up for the night at St. Anne's, and there another notable thing occurred. Their host was a hardened
Creole, and at supper he ate cayenne pepper with a
spoon. Not ordinary cayenne pepper, mind, such as is
sold in shops, which is heavily adulterated with logwood;
but the far fierier pure original. This indeed was an Event
of the first water: none of them ever forgot it.

The desolation through which they drove is indescrib-
able. Tropical scenery is anyhow tedious, prolific, and
gross: the greens more or less uniform; great tubular
stems supporting thick leaves. No tree has an outline because it is crushed up against something else—no *room*.
In Jamaica this profusion swarms over the very mountain ranges: and even the peaks are so numerous that on
the top of one you are surrounded by others, and can see
nothing. There are hundreds of flowers. Then imagine all
this luxuriance smashed, as with a pestle and mortar
—crushed, pulped, and already growing again! Mr. Thornton and his wife were ready to shout with relief when
they caught their first glimpse of the sea, and at last came
out in view of the whole beautiful sweep of Montego Bay
itself.

In the open sea there was a considerable swell, but
within the shelter of the coral reef, with its pinhole en-
trance, all was still as a mirror, where three ships of different sizes lay at anchor, the whole of each beautiful
machine repeated in the water under it. Within the Roads
lay the Bogue Islands; and immediately to the left of the
islands, in the low land at the base of the hills, was the
mouth of a small river—swampy, and (Mr. Thornton informed John) infested with crocodiles. The children had
never seen a crocodile, and hoped one might venture as

far as the town, where they presently arrived: but none did. It was with considerable disappointment that they found they were to go on board the barque at once; for they still hoped that round some corner of the street a crocodile might yet appear.

The *Clorinda* had let go her anchor in six fathoms: the water so clear, and the light so bright, that as they drew near the reflection suddenly disappeared, and instead they found themselves looking right underneath her and out the other side. The refraction made her seem as flat-bellied as a turtle, as if practically all of her were above the surface: and the anchor on its cable seemed to stream out flatly, like a downwards kite, twisting and twining (owing to the undulating surface) in the writhing coral.

This was the only impression Emily retained of going on board the ship: but the ship itself was a strange enough object, requiring all her attention. John was the only one who could remember the journey out at all clearly. Emily thought she could, but was really only remembering her visualisations of what she had been told: in fact, she found that a real ship was totally unlike the thing she thought she remembered.

By some last whim of the captain's the shrouds were being set up—tauter than seemed good to the sailors, who grumbled as they strained the creaking lanyards. John did not envy them, winding away at that handle in the hot sun: but he did envy the chap whose job it was to dip his hand in a great pot of aromatic Stockholm tar and work it into the deadeyes. He was tarred up to the elbows, and John itched to be so too.

In a moment the children were scattered all over the ship, smelling here, miaowing, sniffing there, like cats in a new home. Mr. and Mrs. Thornton stood by the main companionway, a little disconsolate at their children's happy preoccupation, a little regretting the lack of proper emotional scene.

"I think they will be happy here, Frederic," said Mrs. Thornton. "I wish we could have afforded to send them by the steamboat: but children find amusement even in discomfort."

Mr. Thornton grunted.

"I wish schools had never been invented!" he suddenly burst out: "They wouldn't then be so indispensable!"

There was a short pause for the logic of this to cross the footlights: then he went on:

"I know what will happen; they'll come away . . . *mugs!* Just ordinary little mugs, like anyone else's brats! I'm dashed if I don't think a hundred hurricanes would be better than that."

Mrs. Thornton shuddered: but she continued bravely:

"You know, I think they were getting almost *too* devoted to us? We have been such an unrivalled centre of their lives and thoughts. It doesn't do for minds developing to be completely dependent on one person."

Captain Marpole's grizzled head emerged from the scuttle. A sea-dog: clear blue eyes of a translucent truthworthiness: a merry, wrinkled, morocco-coloured face: a rumbling voice.

"He's too good to be true," whispered Mrs. Thornton.

"Not at all! It's a sophism to imagine people don't conform to type!" barked Mr. Thornton. He felt at sixes and sevens.

Captain Marpole certainly looked the ideal Children's Captain. He would, Mrs. Thornton decided, be careful without being fussy—for she was all in favour of courageous gymnastics, though glad she would not have to witness them herself. Captain Marpole cast his eyes benignantly over the swarming imps.

"They'll worship him," she whispered to her husband. (She meant, of course, that he would worship them.) It was an important point, this, of the captain: important as the personality of a headmaster.

"So that's the nursery, eh?" said the captain, crushing Mrs. Thornton's hand. She strove to answer, but found her throat undoubtedly paralysed. Even Mr. Thornton's ready tongue was at a loss. He looked hard at the captain, jerked his thumb towards the children, wrestled in his mind with an elaborate speech, and finally enunciated in a small, unlikely voice:

"Smack 'em."

Then the captain had to go about his duties: and for an hour the father and mother sat disconsolately on the main hatch, quite deserted. Even when all was ready for departure it was impossible to muster the flock for a collective goodbye.

Already the tug was fulminating in its gorge, and ashore they must go. Only Emily and John had been captured, and stood talking uneasily to their parents, as if to strangers, using only a quarter of their minds. With a rope to be climbed dangling before his very nose, John simply did not know how this delay was to be supported, and lapsed into complete silence.

"Time to go ashore, Ma'am," said the captain: "we must be off now."

Very formally the two generations kissed each other, and said farewell. Indeed the elders were already at the gangway before the meaning of it all dawned in Emily's head. She rushed after her mother, gripped her ample flesh in two strong fists, and sobbed and wept. "Come, too, Mother, oh, do come too!"

Honestly, it had only occurred to her that very moment
that this was a *parting*.

"But think what an adventure it will be," said Mrs.
Thornton bravely, "much more than if I came too! You'll
have to look after the Liddlies, just as if you were a real
grownup!"

"But I don't want any more adventures!" sobbed Emily:
"I've *got* an *Earthquake!*"

Passions were running far too high for anyone to be
aware how the final separation took place. The next thing
Mrs. Thornton could remember was how tired her arm
had been, after waving and waving at that dwindling
speck which bore away on the land breeze, hung awhile
stationary in the intervening calm, then won the trade
and climbed up into the blue.

Meanwhile, at the rail stood Margaret Fernandez, who,
with her little brother Harry, was going to England by the
same boat. No one had come to see them off: and the
brown nurse who was accompanying them had gone
below the moment she came on board, so as to be ill as
quickly as possible. How handsome Mr. Bas-Thornton
had looked, with his English distinction! Yet everyone
knew he had no money. Her set white face was turned
towards the land, her chin quivering at intervals. Slowly
the harbour disappeared: the disordered profligacy of the
turbulent, intricate mass of hills sank lower in the sky.
The occasional white houses, and white puffs of steam
and smoke from the sugar-mills, vanished. At last the
land, all palely shimmering like the bloom on grapes, settled down into the mirror of emerald and blue.

She wondered whether the Thornton children would
prove companionable or a nuisance. They were all younger
than she was, which was a pity.

2

On the journey back to Ferndale both father and mother were silent, actuated by that tug of jealousy against sympathy which a strong common emotion begets in familiar rather than passionate companions.

They were above the ordinary sentimentalities of grass-bereavement (above choking over small shoes found in cupboards), but not above a rather strong dose of the natural instincts of parenthood, Frederic no less than his wife.

But when they were nearly home, Mrs. Thornton began to chuckle to herself:

"Funny little thing, Emily! Did you notice almost the last thing she said? She said 'I've got an earthquake.' She must have got it mixed up in her silly old head with earache."

There was a long pause: and then she remarked again:

"John is so much the most sensitive: he was absolutely too full to speak."

3

When they got home it was many days before they could bring themselves openly to mention the children. When some reference had to be made, they spoke round them, in an uncomfortable way, as if they had died.

But after a few weeks they had a most welcome surprise. The *Clorinda* was calling at the Caymans, and taking the Leeward Passage: and while riding off the Grand Cayman Emily and John wrote letters, and a vessel bound for Kingston had taken charge of them and eventually they reached Ferndale. It had not even occurred to either parent that this would be possible.

This was Emily's:

MY DEAR PARENTS,

This ship is full of Turtles. We stopped here and they came out in boats. There is turtles in the saloon under the tables for you to put your feet on, and turtles in the passages and on the deck, and everywhere you go. The captain says we mustn't fall overboard now because his boats are full of turtles too, with water. The sailors bring the others on deck every day to have a wash and when you stand them up they look just as if they had pinafores on. They make such a funny sighing and groaning in the night, at first I thought it was everybody being ill, but you get used to it, it is just like people being ill.

Your loving daughter,

EMILY

And John's:

MY DEAREST PARENTS,

The captain's son Henry is a wonderful chap, he goes up the rigging with his hands alone, he is ever so strong. He can turn round under a bellying pin without touching the deck, I can't but I hang from the ratlines by my heels which the sailors say is very brave, but they don't like Emily doing it, funny. I hope you are both in excellent health, one of the sailors has a monkey but its tail is Sore.

Your affectionate son,

JOHN

That was the last news they could expect for many months. The *Clorinda* was not touching anywhere else. It gave Mrs. Thornton a cold feeling in the stomach to measure just *how* long. But she argued, logically enough, that the time must come to an end, all time does: there is nothing so inexorable as a ship, plodding away, plodding away, all over the place, till at last it quite certainly reaches that small speck on the map which all the time it had intended to reach. Philosophically speaking, a ship in its port of departure is just as much in its port of arrival: two point-events differing in time and place, but not in degree of reality. *Ergo*, that first letter from England was as good as written, only not quite . . . legible yet. And the same applied to seeing them. (But here one must stop, for the same argument applied to old age and death, it wouldn't do.)

Yet, a bare fortnight after the arrival of this first budget, still another letter arrived, from Havana. The *Clorinda* had put in there unexpectedly, it appeared: the letter was from Captain Marpole.

"What a dear man he is," said Alice. "He must have known how anxious we would be for every scrap of news."

Captain Marpole's letter was not so terse and vivid as the children's had been; still, for the news it contained, I give it in full:

HAVANA DE CUBA

HONOURED SIR AND MADAM,

I hasten to write to you to relieve you of any uncertainty!

After leaving the Caymans we stood for the Leeward Passage, and sighted the Isle of Pines and False Cape on the morning of the 19th and Cape S. Antonio in the evening, but were prevented from rounding the same by a true Norther, the first of the season, on the 22nd, however, the wind coming round sufficiently we rounded the cape in a lively fashion and stood N½E well away from the Coloradoes which are a dangerous reef lying off this part of the Cuban coast. At six o'clock on the morning of the 23rd there being light airs only I sighted three sail in the North East, evidently merchantmen bound on the same course as ourselves, at the same time a schooner of similar character was observed standing out towards us from the direction of Black Key, and I pointed her out to my mate just before going below, having the wind of us he was within hailing distance by ten in the morning, judge then of our astonishment when he rudely opened ten or twelve disguised gunports and unmasked a whole broadside of artillery trained upon us, ordering us at the same time in the most peremptory manner to heave-to or he would sink us instanter. There was nothing to do but to comply although considering the friendly relations at present existing between the English and all other governments my mate was quite at a loss to account for his action, and imagined it due to a mistake which would be speedily explained, we were immediately boarded by about fifty or seventy ruffians of the worst Spanish type, armed with knives and cutlasses, who took possession of the ship and confined me in my cabin and my mate and crew forward while they ransacked the vessel committing every possible excess broaching rum-casks and breaking the necks off wine-bottles and soon a great number of them were lying about the deck in an intoxicated condition, their leader then informed me he was aware I had a considerable sum in specie on board and used *every possible threat which villainy could devise* to make me disclose its hiding-place, it was useless for me to assure him that beyond the fifty or so pounds they had already discovered I carried none, he grew even more insistent in his demands, declaring that his information was certain, tearing down the paneling in my cabin in his search. He carried off my instruments, my clothes, and all my personal possessions, even taking from me the poor Locket in which I was used to carry the portrait of my Wife, and no appeal to his sensibility, tho' I shed tears, would make him return this to him worthless object, he also tore down and carried away the cabin bell-pulls, which could be of no possible use to him and was an act of the most open *piracy*, at length, seeing I was obdurate, he threatened to blow up the ship *and all in it* if I would not yield, he prepared the train and would have proceeded to carry out this devilish threat if I had not in this last extremity, consented.

I come now to the latter part of my tale. The children had

taken refuge in the deck-house and had been up to now free
from harm, except for a cuff or two and the Degrading Sights
they must have witnessed, but no sooner was the specie some
five thousand pounds in all mostly my private property and
most of our cargo (chiefly rum sugar coffee and arrowroot)
removed to the schooner than her captain, in sheer infamous
wantonness, had them all brought out from their refuge your
own little ones and the two Fernandez children who were also
on board and murdered them, every one. That anything so
wicked should look like a man I should not have believed, had
I been told, tho' I have lived long and seen all kinds of men, I
think he is mad; indeed I am sure of it; and I take Oath that he
shall be brought to at least that tithe of justice which is in
Human hands, for two days we drifted about in a helpless
condition, for our rigging had all been cut, and at last fell in
with an American man-of-war, who gave us some assistance,
and would have proceeded in pursuit of the miscreants himself
had he not most explicit orders to elsewhere. I then put in to
the port of Havana, where I informed the correspondent of
Lloyds, the government, and the representative of the *Times*
newspaper, and take the opportunity of writing you this melancholy letter before proceeding to England.

There is one point on which you will still feel some anxiety, considering the sex of some of the poor innocents, and on
which I am glad to be able to set your minds at rest, the
children were taken onto the other vessel in the evening and I
am glad to say there done to death *immediately*, and their
little bodies cast into the sea, as I saw with great relief with my
own eyes. There was no time for what you might fear to have
occurred, and this consolation I am glad to be able to give you.

> I have the honour to be
> Your obedient servant,
> JAS. MARPOLE,
> Master, barque *Clorinda*

CHAPTER THREE

The passage from Montego Bay to the Caymans, where the children had written their letters, is only a matter of a few hours: indeed, in clear weather one can look right across from Jamaica to the peak of Tarquinio in Cuba.

There is no harbour: and the anchorage, owing to the reefs and ledges, is difficult. The *Clorinda* brought up off the Grand Cayman, the look-out man in the chains feeling his way to a white, sandy patch of bottom which affords the only safe resting-place there: and causing the anchor to be let go to windward of it. Luckily, the weather was fine.

The island, a longish one at the western end of the group, is low, and covered with palms. Presently a succession of boats brought out a quantity of turtles, as Emily described. The natives also brought parrots to sell to the sailors: but failed to dispose of many.

At last, however, the uncomfortable Caymans were left behind, and they set their course towards the Isle of

Pines, a large island in a gulf of the Cuban coast. One of
the sailors, called Curtis, had once been wrecked there,
and was full of stories about it. It is a very unpleasant
place; sparsely inhabited, and covered with labyrinthine
woods. The only food available is a kind of tree. There is
also a species of bean which looks tempting: but it is
deadly poison. The crocodiles, Curtis said, were so fierce
they chased him and his companions into trees: the only
way to escape from them was to throw them your cap to
worry: or if you were bold, to disable them with a blow of
a stick on the loins. There were also a great many snakes,
including a kind of boa.

The current off the Isle of Pines sets strongly to the
east: so the *Clorinda* kept close inshore, to cheat it. They
passed Cape Corrientes—looking, when first sighted, like
two hummocks in the sea: they passed Holandes Point,
known as False Cape San Antonio: but were prevented for
some time, as Captain Marpole told in his letter, from
rounding the true one. For to attempt Cape San Antonio
in a Norther is to waste your labour.

They lay-to in sight of that long, low, rocky, treeless
promontory in which the great island of Cuba terminates,
and waited. They were so close that the fisherman's hut
on its southern side was clearly discernible.

For the children, those first few days at sea had flashed
by like a kind of prolonged circus. There is no machine
invented for sober purposes so well adapted also to play
as the rigging of a ship: and the kindly captain, as Mrs.
Thornton had divined, was willing to give them a lot of
freedom. First came the climbing of a few rungs of the
ratlines in a sailor's charge: higher each time, till John
attained a gingerly touching of the yard, then hugged it,
then straddled it. Soon, running up the ratlines and pranc-

ing on the yard (as if it were a mere table-top) had no
further thrill for John or Emily either. (To go out on the
yard was not allowed.)

But when the ratlines had palled, the most lasting joy
undoubtedly lay in that network of foot-ropes and chains
and stays which spreads out under and on each side of the
bowsprit. Here, familiarity only bred content. Here, in
fine weather, one could climb or be still: stand, sit, hang,
swing, or lie: now this end up, now that: and all with the
cream of the blue sea being whipt up for one's own especial pleasure, almost within touching distance: and the
big white wooden lady (*Clorinda* herself), bearing the
whole vessel so lightly on her back, her knees in the hubble-bubble, her cracks almost filled up with so much
painting, vaster than any living lady, as a constant and
unannoying companion.

In the midst there was a kind of spear, its haft set
against the underside of the bowsprit, its point perpendic-
ularly down towards the water—the dolphin-striker. Here
it was that the old monkey (who had the Sore tail) loved
to hang, by the mere stub which was all a devouring can-
cer had left him, chattering to the water. He took no notice of the children, nor they of him: but both parties
grew attached to each other, for all that.

——How small the children all looked, on a ship, when
you saw them beside the sailors! It was as if they were a
different order of beings! Yet they were living creatures
just the same, full of promise.

John, with his downy, freckled face, and general round
energeticalness.

Emily, with her huge palm-leaf hat, and colourless cotton frock tight over her minute impish erect body: her
thin, almost expressionless face: her dark grey eyes con-

tracted to escape the blaze, yet shining as it were in spite of themselves: and her really beautiful lips, that looked almost as if they were sculptured.

Margaret Fernandez, taller (as midgets go: she was just thirteen), with her square white face and tangled hair, her elaboratish clothes.

Her little brother *Harry*, by some throwback for all the world like a manikin Spaniard.

And the smaller Thorntons: *Edward*, mouse-coloured, with a general mousy (but pleasing) expression: *Rachel*, with tight short gold curls and a fat pink face (John's colouring watered down): and last of all *Laura*, a queer mite of three with heavy dark eyebrows, and blue eyes, a big head-top and a receding chin—as if the Procreative Spirit was getting a little hysterical by the time it reached her. A silver-age conception, Laura's, decidedly.

When the norther blew itself out, it soon fell away almost dead calm. The morning they finally rounded Cape San Antonio was hot, blazing hot. But it is never stuffy at sea: there is only this disadvantage, that while on land a shady hat protects you from the sun, at sea nothing can protect you from that second sun which is mirrored upwards from the water, strikes under all defences, and burns the unseasoned skin from all your undersides. Poor John! His throat and chin were a blistered red.

From the point itself there is a whitish bank in two fathoms, bowed from north to northeast. The outer side is clean and steep-to, and in fine weather one can steer along it by eye. It ends in Black Key, a rock standing out of the water like a ship's hull. Beyond that lies a channel, very foul and difficult to navigate: and beyond that again the Coloradoes Reef begins, the first of a long chain of reefs following the coast in a north-easterly direction as far as Honde Bay, two-thirds the way to Havana. Within these reefs lies the intricate Canal de Guaniguanico (of which this channel is the westernmost outlet) with its own rather dubious little ports. But ocean traffic, needless to say, shuns the whole box of tricks: and the *Clorinda* advisedly stood well away to the northward, keeping her course at a gentle amble for the open Atlantic.

John was sitting outside the galley with the sailor called Curtis, who was instructing him in the neat mystery of a Turk's-head. Young Henry Marpole was steering. Emily was messing around—not talking, just being by him.

As for the other sailors, they were all congregated in a ring, up in the bows, so that one saw nothing but their backs. But every now and then a general guffaw, and a sudden surging of the whole group, showed they were up to something or other.

John presently tiptoed forward, to see what it might be. He thrust his bullet-head among their legs, and worked his way in till he had as good a view as the earliest comer.

He found they had got the old monkey, and were filling him up with rum. First they gave him biscuit soaked in it: then they dipped rags in a pannikin of the stuff, and squeezed them into his mouth. Then they tried to make him drink direct; but that he would not do—it only wasted a lot of spirit.

John felt a vague horror at all this: though of course he did not guess the purpose behind it.

The poor brute shivered and chattered, rolled his eyes, spluttered. I suppose it must have been an excruciatingly funny sight. Every now and then he would seem altogether overcome by the spirit. Then one of the sailors would lay him on the top of an old beef barrel—but hey presto, he would be up like lightning, trying to streak through the air over their heads. But he was no bird; they caught him each time, and set to work to dope him again.

As for John, he could no more have left the scene now than Jacko the monkey could.

It was astonishing what a lot of spirit the wizened little brute could absorb. He was drunk, of course: hopelessly, blindly, madly drunk. But he was not paralytic, not even somnolent: and it seemed as if nothing could overcome him. So at last they gave up the attempt. They fetched a wooden box, and cut a notch in the edge. Then they put him on the barrel-top, and clapt the box over him, and after much maneuvering his gangrenous tail was made to come out through the notch. Anaesthetised or not, the operation on him was to proceed. John stared, transfixed, at that obscene wriggling stump which was all one could see of the animal: and out of the corner of his eye he could see at the same time the uproarious operators, the tar-stained knife.

But the moment the blade touched flesh, with an awful screech the mommet contrived to fling off his cage—leapt on the surgeon's head—leapt from there high in the air— caught the forestay—and in a twinkling was away and up high in the fore-rigging.

Then began the hue and cry. Sixteen men flinging about in lofty acrobatics, all to catch one poor old drunk monkey. For he was drunk as a lord, and sick as a cat. His course varied between wild and hair-raising leaps (a sort of inspired gymnastics) and doleful incompetent reelings on a taut rope which threatened at every moment to catapult him into the sea. But even so they could never quite catch him.

No wonder that all the children, now, stood open-mouthed and open-eyed on the deck beneath in the sun till their necks nearly broke—*such* a Free Fun Fair and Circus!

And no wonder that on that passenger-schooner which Marpole, before going below, had sighted drifting toward them from the direction of the Black Key channel the ladies had left the shade of the awning and were crowding at the rail, parasols twirling, lorgnettes and opera-glasses in action, all twittering like a cage of linnets. Just too far off to distinguish the tiny quarry, they might well have wondered what sort of a bedlam-vessel of sea-acrobats the light easterly air was bearing them down upon.

They were so interested that presently a boat was hoisted out, and the ladies—and some gentlemen as well —crowded into it.

Poor little Jacko missed his hold at last: fell plump on the deck and broke his neck. That was the end of him— and of the hunt too, of course. The aerial ballet was over, in its middle, with no final tableau. The sailors began, in twos and threes, to slide to the deck.

But the visitors were already on board.

That is how the *Clorinda* really was taken. There was no display of artillery—but then, Captain Marpole could hardly know this, seeing he was below in his bunk at the time. Henry was steering by that sixth sense which only comes into operation when the other five are asleep. The mate and crew had been so intent on what they were doing that the *Flying Dutchman* himself might have laid alongside for all they cared.

2

Indeed, the whole maneuver was executed so quietly that Captain Marpole never even woke—incredible though this will seem to a seaman. But then, Marpole had begun life as a successful coal merchant.

The mate and crew were bundled into the fo'c'sle (the fox-hole, the children thought it was called), and confined there, the scuttle being secured with a couple of nails.

The children themselves were shepherded, as related, into the deck-house, where the chairs, and perfectly useless pieces of old rope, and broken tools, and dried-up paint pots were kept, without taking alarm. But the door was immediately shut on them. They had to wait for hours and hours before anything else happened—nearly all day, in fact: and they got very bored, and rather cross.

The actual number of the men who had effected the capture cannot have been more than eight or nine, most of them "women" at that, and not armed—at least with any visible weapon. But a second boatload soon followed them from the schooner. These, for form's sake, were armed with muskets. But there was no possible resistance to fear. Two long nails through the scuttle can secure any number of men pretty effectually.

With this second boatload came both the captain and the mate. The former was a clumsy great fellow, with a sad, silly face. He was bulky, yet so ill-proportioned one got no impression of power. He was modestly dressed in a drab shore-going suit: he was newly shaven, and his sparse hair was pomaded so that it lay in a few dark ribbons across his baldish head-top. But all this shore-decency of appearance only accentuated his big splodgy brown hands, stained and scarred and corned with his calling. Moreover, instead of boots he wore a pair of gigantic heelless slippers in the Moorish manner, which he must have sliced with a knife out of some pair of dead sea-boots. Even his great spreading feet could hardly keep them on, so that he was obliged to walk at the slowest of shuffles, flop-flop along the deck. He stooped, as if always afraid of banging his head on something, and carried the backs of his hands forward, like an orang-outang.

Meanwhile the men set to work methodically but very quietly to remove the wedges that held the battens of the hatches, getting ready to haul up the cargo.

Their leader took several turns up and down the deck before he seemed able to make up his mind to the interview: then lowered himself into Marpole's cabin, followed by his mate.

This mate was a small man: very fair, and intelligent-looking beside his chief. He was almost dapper, in a quiet way, in his dress.

They found Captain Marpole even now only half awake; and the stranger stood for a moment in silence, nervously twiddling his cap in his hands. When he spoke at last, it was with a soft German accent:

"Excuse me," he began, "but would you have the goodness to lend me a few stores?"

Captain Marpole stared in astonishment, first at him and then at the much bepainted faces of the "ladies" pressed against his cabin skylight.

"Who the devil are you?" he contrived to ask at last.

"I hold a commission in the Columbian navy," the stranger explained: "and I am in need of a few stores."

(Meanwhile his men had the hatches off, and were preparing to help themselves to everything in the ship.)

Marpole looked him up and down. It was barely conceivable that even the Columbian navy should have such a figure of an officer. Then his eye wandered back to the skylight.

"If you call yourself a man-of-war, Sir, who in Heaven's name are *those?*" As he pointed, the smirking faces hastily retreated.

The stranger blushed.

"They are rather difficult to explain," he admitted ingenuously.

"If you had said *Turkish* navy, that would have been more reasonable-sounding," said Marpole.

But the stranger did not seem to take the joke. He stood, silent, in a characteristic attitude: rocking himself from foot to foot, and rubbing his cheek on his shoulder.

Suddenly Marpole's ear caught the muffled racketing forward. Almost at the same time a bump that shivered the whole barque told that the schooner had been laid alongside.

"What's that?" he exclaimed. "Is there someone in my hold?"

"Stores . . ." mumbled the stranger.

Marpole up to now had lain growling in his bunk like a dog in its kennel. Now for the first time realising that something serious was afoot, he flung himself out and made for the companionway. The little silent fair man tripped him up, and he fell against the table.

"You had much better stay here, yes?" said the big man. "My fellows shall keep a tally. You shall be paid in full for everything we take."

The eyes of the marine coal-merchant gleamed momentarily:

"You'll have to pay for this outrage to a pretty tune!" he growled.

"I will pay you," said the stranger, with a sudden magnificence in his voice, "at the very least five thousand pounds!"

Marpole stared in astonishment.

"I will write you an order on the Columbian government for that amount," the other went on.

Marpole thumped the table, almost speechless:

"D'you think I believe that cock-and-bull story?" he thundered.

Captain Jonsen made no protest.

"Do you realise that you are technically guilty of *piracy*, making a forced requisition on a British ship like this, even if you pay every farthing?"

Still Jonsen made no reply, though the bored expression of his mate was lit up for a moment by a smile.

"You'll pay me in *cash!*" Marpole concluded. Then he went off on a fresh tack: "Though how the devil you got on board without my being called beats me! Where's my mate?"

Jonsen began in a toneless voice, as if by rote: "I will write you an order for five thousand pounds: three thousand for the stores, and two thousand you will give me in money."

"We know you've got specie on board," interjected the little fair mate, speaking for the first time.

"Our information is certain!" declared Jonsen.

Marpole at last went white and began to sweat. It took even Fear an extraordinarily long time to penetrate his thick skull. But he denied that he had any treasure on board.

"Is that your answer?" said Jonsen. He drew a heavy pistol from his side pocket: "If you do not tell us the truth, your life shall pay the forfeit." His voice was peculiarly gentle, and mechanical, as if he did not attach much meaning to what he said: "Do not expect mercy, for this is my profession, and in it I am inured to blood."

A frightful squawking from the deck above told Marpole that his chickens were being moved to new quarters.

In an agony of feeling Marpole told him that he had a wife and children, who would be left destitute if his life was taken.

Jonsen, with a rather perplexed look on his face, put the gun back in his pocket, and the two of them began searching for themselves, at the same time stripping the saloon and cabins of everything they contained: firearms, wearing apparel, the bedclothes, and even (as Marpole with a rare touch of accuracy mentioned in his report) the bell-pulls.

Overhead there was a continuous bumping: the rolling of casks, cases, etc.

"Remember," Jonsen went on over his shoulder while he searched, "money cannot recall life, nor in the least avail you when you are dead. If you regard your life in the least, at once acquaint me with the hiding-place, and your life shall be safe."

Marpole's only reply was again to invoke the thought of his wife and children (he was, as a matter of fact, a widower: and his only relative, a niece, would be the better off by his death to the tune of some ten thousand pounds).

But this reiteration seemed to give the mate an idea, and he began to talk to his chief rapidly in a language Marpole had never even heard. For a moment a curious glint came into Jonsen's eye: but soon he was chuckling in the sentimentalest manner, and rubbing his hands.

The mate went on deck to prepare things.

Marpole had no inkling of what was afoot. The mate

went on deck to prepare his plan, whatever it was: and Jonsen busied himself with a last futile search for the hiding-place, in silence.

Presently the mate shouted down to him, and he ordered Marpole on deck.

Poor Marpole groaned. Unloading cargo is inclined to be a messy business anyway: but these visitors had been none too careful. There is no smell in the world worse than when molasses and bilge-water marry: now it was let loose like ten thousand devils. His heart almost broke when he saw the havoc that had been made with the cargo: broken cases, casks, bottles, all about the deck: everything in the greatest confusion: tarpaulins cut to pieces: hatches broken.

From the deck-house came the piercing voice of Laura:
"I want to come out!"

The Spanish "ladies" seemed to have returned to the schooner. His own men were shut up in the fo'c'sle. It was obvious where all the children were, for Laura was not the only vociferator. But the only persons to be seen were six members of the visiting crew, who stood in a line, facing the deck-house, a musket apiece.

It was the little mate who now took charge of the situation:

"Where is your specie hid, Captain?"

The musketeers having their backs to him, "Go to the devil!" replied Marpole.

A startling volley rang out: six neat holes were punctured in the top of the deck-house.

"Hi! Steady there, what are you doing?" John cried out, indignantly, from within.

"If you refuse to tell us, next time their aim will be a foot lower."

"You fiends!" cried Marpole.

"Will you tell me?"

"*No!*"

"*Fire!*"

The second row of holes can only have missed the taller children by a few inches.

There was a moment's silence: then a sudden wild shriek from within the deck-house. It was so terrified a sound not their own mothers could have told which throat it came from. One only, though.

The stranger-captain had been slouching about in an agitated way: but at that shriek he turned on Marpole, his face purple with a sudden fury:

"*Now* will you say?"

But Marpole was now completely master of himself. He did not hesitate:

"NO!"

"Next time he gives the order it will be to shoot right through their little bodies!"

So that was what Marpole had meant in his letter by "*every possible threat which villainy could devise*"!

But even by this he was not to be daunted:

"No, I tell you!"

Heroic obstinacy!

But instead of giving the fatal order, Jonsen lifted a paw like a bear's, and banged Marpole's jaw with it. The latter fell to the deck, stunned.

It was then they took the children out of the deck-house.

They were not really much frightened: except Margaret, who did seem to be taking it all to heart rather. Being shot at is so unlike what one expects it to be that one can hardly connect the two ideas enough to have the

appropriate emotions, the first few times. It is not half so
startling as someone jumping out on you with a *"Boo!"* in
the dark, for instance. The boys were crying a little: the
girls were hot and cross and hungry.)

"What were you doing?" Rachel asked, brightly, of one
of the firing-party.

But only t.e captain and the mate could speak English.
The latter, ignoring Rachel's question, explained that they
were all to go on board the schooner—"to have some supper," he said.

He had all a sailor's reassuring charm of manner. Under
the charge of two Spanish seamen they were helped over
the bulwarks onto the smaller vessel, which was just cast-
ing off.

There the strange sailors broke open a whole case of
crystallised fruits, on which they might turn the edge of
their long appetites as much as they could.

When poor stunned Captain Marpole came to his
senses, it was to find himself tied to the mainmast. Several
handfuls of shavings and splintered wood were piled
round his feet, and Jonsen was sprinkling them plentifully
with gun-powder—though not perhaps enough, it is true,
to "blow up the ship and all in it."

The small fair mate stood at hand in the gathering dusk
with a lighted torch, ready to fire the pyre.

What could a man do in such straits? At that dreadful
moment, the old fellow had to admit that he was beaten
at last. He told them where his freight-money—some
£900—was hidden: and they let him go.

Just as the darkness closed in, the last of the pirates
returned to their ship. Not a sound was to be heard of the
children: but Marpole guessed that they had been taken
there too.

Before releasing his crew he lit a lantern, and began a sort of inventory of what was gone. It was heart-breaking enough: besides the cargo, all his spare sails, cordage, provisions, guns, paint, powder; all his wearing apparel, and that of his mates: all nautical instruments gone, cabin stores—the saloon in fact gutted of everything, not even a knife or spoon left, tea or sugar, nor a second shirt to his back left. Only the children's luggage was left untouched: and the turtles. Their melancholy sighing was the sole sound to be heard.

But it was almost as heart-breaking to see what the pirates had *left:* anything damaged, such worn-out and useless gear as he had been only waiting for some "storm" to wash overboard—not one of these eyesores was missing.

What, in Heaven's name, was the use of an insurance policy? He began to collect the rubbish himself, and dump it over the side.

But Captain Jonsen saw him:

"Hi!" he shouted: "You dirty svindler! I will write to Lloyds and expose you! I will write myself!" He was horribly shocked at the other's dishonesty.

So Marpole had to give it up, for the time at any rate. He took a spike and broke open the fo'c'sle, and as well, as the sailors found Margaret's brown nurse. She had hidden there the whole day, probably from motives of fright.

3

You would have thought that supper on the schooner that night would have been a hilarious affair. But, somehow, it was *manqué.*

A prize of such value had naturally put the crew in the best of humours: and a meal which consisted mainly

of crystallised fruit, followed as an afterthought by bread
and chopped onions served in one enormous communal
bowl, eaten on the open deck under the stars after bed-
time, should have done the same by the children. But
nevertheless both parties were seized by a sudden, overpowering, and most unexpected fit of shyness. Consequently no state banquet was ever so formal, or so boring.

I suppose it was the lack of a common language which
first generated the infection. The Spanish sailors, used
enough to this difficulty, grinned, pointed, and bobbed:
but the children retired into a display of good manners
which it would certainly have surprised their parents to
see. Whereon the sailors become equally formal: and
one poor monkeyfied little fellow who by nature belched
continually was so benudged and bewinked by his companions, and so covered in confusion of his own accord,
that presently he went away to eat by himself. Even then,
so silent was this revel, he could still be heard faintly
belching, half the ship's length away.

Perhaps it would have gone better if the captain and
mate had been there, with their English. But they were
too busy, looking over the personal belongings they had
brought from the barque, sorting out by the light of a
lantern anything too easily identifiable and reluctantly
committing it to the sea.

It was at the loud splashes made by a couple of empty
trunks, stamped in large letters JAS MARPOLE, that they
heard a roar of unassumed indignation arise from the
neighbouring barque. The two paused in their work,
astonished: why should a crew already spoiled of all they
possessed take it so hardly when one heaved a couple of
old worthless trunks into the sea?

It was inexplicable.

They continued their task, taking no further notice of the *Clorinda*.

Once supper was over, the social situation became even more awkward. The children stood about, not knowing what to do with their hands, or even their legs: unable to talk to their hosts, and feeling it would be rude to talk to one another: wishing badly that it was time to leave. If only it had been light they could have been happy enough exploring: but in the darkness there was nothing to do, nothing whatever.

The sailors soon found occupations of their own: and the captain and mate, as I have said, were already busy.

Once the sorting was over, however, there was nothing for Jonsen to do except return the children to the barque, and get well clear while the breeze and the darkness lasted.

But on hearing those splashes, Marpole's lively imagination had interpreted them in his own way. They suggested that there was now no reason to wait: indeed, every reason to be gone.

I think he was quite honestly misled.

It was after all but a small slip to say he had "seen with his own eyes" what he had heard with his own ears: and the intention was pious.

He set his men feverishly to work; and when Captain Jonsen looked his way again, the *Clorinda,* with every stitch spread in the starlight, was already half a mile to leeward.

To pursue her, right in the track of shipping, was out of the question. Jonsen had to content himself with staring after her through his night-glass.

4

Captain Jonsen set the little monkeyfied sailor, who had been so mortified earlier in the evening, to clear the schooner's fore-hold. The warps and brooms and fenders it contained were piled to one side, and a sufficiency of bed-clothes for the guests was provided from the plunder.

But nothing could now thaw them. They clambered down the ladder and received their blanket apiece in an uncomfortable silence. Jonsen hung about, anxious to be helpful in this matter of getting into beds which were not there, but not knowing how to set about it. So he gave it up at last, and swung himself up through the fore hatch, talking to himself.

The last they saw of him was his fantastic slippers, hanging each from a big toe, outlined against the stars: but it never entered their heads to laugh.

Once, however, the familiar comfort of a blanket under their chins had begun to have its effect, and they were obviously quite alone, a little life did begin to return into these dumb statues.

The darkness was profound, only accentuated by the starlit square of the open hatchway. First the long silence was broken by someone turning over, almost freely. Then presently:

LAURA (*in slow, sepulchral tones*): I don't like this bed.
RACHEL (*ditto*): I do.
LAURA: It's a horrid bed; there isn't any!
EMILY }
JOHN } : Sh! Go to sleep!
EDWARD: I smell cockroaches.
EMILY: Sh!

EDWARD (*loudly and hopefully*): They'll bite our nails off, because we haven't washed, and our skin, and our hair, and ——

LAURA: There's a cockroach in my bed! Get out!

(*You could hear the brute go zooming away. But* LAURA *was already out too.*)

EMILY: Laura! Go back to bed!

LAURA: I can't when there's a cockroach in it!

JOHN: Get into bed again, you little fool! He's gone long ago!

LAURA: But I expect he has left his wife.

HARRY: They don't have wives, they're wives themselves.

RACHEL: Ow! Laura, stop it! Emily, Laura's walking on me!

EMILY: Lau-*rer!*

LAURA: Well, I must walk on something!

EMILY: Go to sleep!

(*Silence for a while.*)

LAURA: I haven't said my prayers.

EMILY: Well, say them lying down.

RACHEL: She mustn't, that's lazy.

JOHN: Shut up, Rachel, she must.

RACHEL: It's wicked! You go to sleep in the middle, then. People who go to sleep in the middle ought to be damned, they ought. Oughtn't they? (*Silence.*) Oughtn't they? (*Still silence.*) Emily, I say, oughtn't they?

JOHN: No!

RACHEL (*dreamily*): I think there's lots more people ought to be damned than are.

(*Silence again.*)

HARRY: Marghie. (*Silence.*) Marghie! (*Silence.*)

JOHN: What's up with Marghie? Won't she speak?

(*A faint sob is heard.*)

HARRY: I don't know.

(*Another sob.*)

JOHN: Is she often like this?

HARRY: She's an awful ass sometimes.

JOHN: Marghie, what's up?

MARGARET (*miserably*): Let me alone!

RACHEL: I believe she's frightened! (*Chants tauntingly.*)
Marghie's got the bogies, the bogies, the bogies!

MARGARET (*sobbing out loud*): Oh you little fools!

JOHN: Well, what's the matter with you, then?

MARGARET (*after a pause*): I'm older than any of you.

JOHN: Well, *that's* a funny reason to be frightened!

MARGARET: It isn't.

JOHN: It is!

MARGARET (*warming to the argument*): It isn't, I tell
you!

JOHN: *It is!*

MARGARET (*smugly*): That's simply because you're all
too young to know. . . .

JOHN: Oh, hit her, Emily!

EMILY (*sleepily*): Hit her yourself.

HARRY: But Marghie, why are we here? (*No answer.*)
Emily, why are we here?

EMILY (*indifferently*): I don't know. I expect they just
wanted to change us.

HARRY: I expect so. But they never *told* us we were
going to be changed.

EMILY: Grownups never *do* tell us things.

CHAPTER FOUR

The children all slept late, and all woke at the same moment as if by clockwork. They sat up, and yawned uniformly, and stretched the stiffness out of their legs and backs (they were lying on solid wood, remember).

The schooner was steady, and people tramping about the deck. The main-hold and fore-hold were all one: and from where they were they could see the main-hatch had been opened. The captain appeared through it legs first, and dropped onto the higgledy-piggledy of the *Clorinda's* cargo.

For some time they simply stared at him. He looked uneasy, and was talking to himself as he tapped now this case with his pencil, now that, and presently shouted rather fiercely to people on deck.

"All right, all right," came from above the injured voice of the mate. "There's no such hurry as all that."

On which the captain's mutterings to himself swelled, as if ten people were conversing at once in his chest.

"May we get up yet?" asked Rachel.

Captain Jonsen spun round—he had forgotten their existence.

"Eh?"

"May we get up, please?"

"You can go to the debble." He muttered this so low the children did not hear it. But it was not lost on the mate.

"Hey! Ey! Ey!" he called down, reprovingly.

"Yes! Get up! Go on deck! Here!" The captain viciously set up a short ladder for them to climb through the hatch.

They were greatly astonished to find the schooner was no longer at sea. Instead, she was snugly moored against a little wooden wharf, in a pleasant land-locked bay; with a pleasant but untidy village, of white wooden houses with palm-leaf roofs, behind it; and the tower of a small sandstone church emerging from the abundant greenery. On the quay were a few well-dressed loungers, watching the preparations for unloading. The mate was directing the labours of the crew, who were rigging the cargo-gaff and getting ready for a hot morning's work.

The mate nodded cheerfully to the children, but thereafter took no notice of them, which was rather mortifying. The truth is that the man was busy.

At the same time there emerged from somewhere aft a collection of the oddest-looking young men. Margaret decided she had never seen such beautiful young men before. They were slim, yet nicely rounded; and dressed in exquisite clothes (if a trifle thread-bare). But their faces! Those beautiful olive-tinted ovals! Those large, black-ringed, soft brown eyes, those unnaturally carmine lips! They minced across the deck, chattering to each other in high-pitched tones, "twittering like a cage of linnets . . ." and made their way on shore.

"Who are they?" Emily asked the captain, who had just re-emerged from below.

"Who are who?" he murmured absently, without looking round: "Oh, those?—Fairies."

"*Hey! Yey! Yey!*" cried the mate, more disapprovingly than ever.

"*Fairies?*" cried Emily in astonishment.

But Captain Jonsen began to blush. He went crimson from the nape of his neck to the bald patches on the top of his head, and left.

"He is *silly!*" said Emily.

"I wonder if we go onto the land yet," said Edward.

"We'd better wait until we're told, hadn't we, Emily?" said Harry.

"I didn't know England would be like this," said Rachel. "It's very like Jamaica."

"This isn't England," said John, "you stupid!"

"But it must be," said Rachel: "England's where we're going."

"We don't get to England yet," said John. "It must be somewhere we're stopping at, like when we got all those turtles."

"I like stopping at places," said Laura.

"I don't," said Rachel.

"I do, though," pursued Laura.

"Where are those young men gone?" Margaret asked the mate. "Are they coming back?"

"They'll just come back to be paid, after we've sold the cargo," he answered.

"Then they're not living on the ship?" she pursued.

"No, we hired them from Havana."

"But what for?"

He looked at her in surprise: "Why, those are the 'la-

dies' we had on board, to look like passengers. You didn't
think they were real ladies, did you?"

"What, were they dressed up?" asked Emily excitedly:
"What fun!"

"I like dressing up," said Laura.

"I don't," said Rachel, "I think it's babyish."

"*I* thought they were real ladies," admitted Emily.

"We're a respectable ship's crew, we are," said the mate,
a trifle stiffly—and without too good logic, when you
come to think of it. "Here, you go on shore and amuse
yourselves."

So the children went ashore, holding hands in a long
row, and promenaded the town in a formal sort of way.
Laura wanted to go off by herself, but the others would
not let her: and when they returned the line was still
unbroken. They had seen all there was to see, and no one
had taken the least notice of them (so far as they were
aware), and they wanted to start asking questions again.

It was, then, a charming little sleepy old place, in its
way, Santa Lucia: isolated on the forgotten western end
of Cuba between Nombre de Dios and the Rio de Puer-
cos: cut off from the open sea by the intricate nature of
the channels through the reefs and the banks of Isabella,
channels only navigable to the practised and creeping
local coasting craft and shunned like poison by bigger
traffic; on land isolated by a hundred miles of forest from
Havana.

Time was, these little ports of the Canal de Guaniguanico had been pretty prosperous, as bases for pirates:
but it was a fleeting prosperity. There came the heroic
attack of an American squadron under Captain Allen, in
1823, on the Bay of Sejuapo, their headquarters. From
that blow (although it took many years to take full

effect) the industry never really recovered: it dwindled
and dwindled, like hand-weaving. One could make money
much faster in a city like Havana, and with less risk (if
less respectably). Piracy had long since ceased to pay,
and should have been scrapped years ago: but a voca-
tional tradition will last on a long time after it has ceased
to be economic, in a decadent form. Now Santa Lucia—
and piracy—continued to exist because they always had;
but for no other reason. Such a haul as the *Clorinda* did
not come but once in a blue moon. Every year the amount
of land under cultivation dwindled, and the pirate schoon-
ers were abandoned to rot against the wharves, or ignomin-
iously sold as traders. The young men left for Havana or
the United States. The maidens yawned. The local gran-
dees increased in dignity as their numbers and property
dwindled: an idyllic, simple-minded country community,
oblivious of the outer world and of its own approaching
oblivion.

"I don't think I should like to live here," John decided
when they got back to the ship.

Meanwhile the cargo had been unloaded onto the
quay: and after the siesta a crowd of about a hundred
people gathered round, poking and discussing. The auction was about to begin. Captain Jonsen tramped about
rather in the way of everybody, but especially annoying
the mate by shouting contrary directions every minute.
The latter had a ledger, and a number of labels with
numbers on them which he was pasting onto the various
bales and packages. The sailors were building a kind of
temporary stage—the thing was to be done in style.

Every moment the crowd increased. Because they all
talked Spanish it was a pantomime to the children: like
puppets acting, not like real people moving and talking.

So they discovered what a fascinating game it is to watch
foreigners, whose very simplest words mean nothing to
you, and try and guess what they are about.

Moreover, these were all such funny-looking people:
they moved about as if they were kings, and spat all the
time, and smoked thin black cigars, the blue smoke of
which ascended from their enormous hats as from censers.

At one moment there was a diversion—the crowd suddenly gaped, and there staggered onto the stage the whole
crew of the schooner carrying a huge pair of scales: it was
always on the point of being too much for them, and running suddenly away with them in another direction.

There were quite a number of ladies in the crowd—old
ones, they seemed to the children. Some were thin and
dried up, like monkeys; but most were fat, and one was
fatter than all of them and treated with the greatest respect (perhaps for her moustache). She was the wife of
the Chief Magistrate: Señora del Ilustrísimo Juzgado del
Municipal de Santa Lucia, to give her her title. She had a
rocking-chair of suitable strength and width, which was
carried by a short squinting Negro and set in the very
middle of the scene, right in front of the platform. There
she throned herself: and the negro stood behind her, holding a violet silk sunshade over her head.

No one can doubt that she would immediately become
the most noticeable thing in the picture.

She had a powerful bass voice, and when she uttered
some jocundity (as she repeatedly did), everyone heard
it, however much they were chattering among themselves.

The children, as was their custom, wormed their way
without any excess of civility through the crowd and
grouped themselves round her throne.

The captain either did not know, or suddenly refused to

know, a single word of Spanish; so the auctioneering devolved on the mate. The latter mounted the stage, and,
with a great assumption of competence, began.

But auctioneering is an art: it is as easy to write a son-
net in a foreign tongue as to conduct a successful auction.
One must have at one's command eloquence without a
hitch: the faculty of kindling an audience, amusing them,
castigating them, converting them, till they rattle out
increments as a camp-meeting rattles out Amens: till they
totally forget the worth (and even the nature) of the lot,
and begin to take a real pride in a long run of bidding—as
a champion does in a long break at billiards.

The little mate had been to a good school, it is true;
for he had once resided in Wales, where one sees auctioneering in its finest flower. In Welsh, or English, or
even in his native tongue, he could have acquitted himself
fairly well; but in Spanish, just that margin of power was
lacking to him. The audience remained stern, cold, criti-
cal, bidding grudgingly.

As if this language difficulty were not in itself enough,
there sat that overpowering old dame on her throne, dis-
tracting with her jokes whatever vestige of attention he
might otherwise have managed to arouse.

When the third lot of coffee came to be dealt with,
there was even the beginning of a rather nasty row. The
children were highly scandalised: they had never seen
grown-ups being rude to one another before. The captain
had undertaken the weighing, and it was something to do
with a habit he had of leaning against the scales while he
read them. Being short-sighted, he could see the figures
much more clearly like that: but it displeased the buyers,
and they had a lot to say about it.

The captain, mortified, wrung his hands, and began to

answer them in Danish. They rejoined in Spanish even
more stingingly. He stumped off in a sulk: they could all
conduct his affairs without him, if they weren't prepared
to treat him with a little consideration.

But who would be less partial? The mate, angry, main-
tained that to elect one of the buyers was equally objec-
tionable.

Thereon an earthquake began in the fat old lady, and
gradually gathered enough force to lift her onto her feet.
She took John by the shoulders, and pushed him before
her to the scales. Then in a few witty, ringing words she
suggested her solution—*he* should do the weighing.

The audience were pleased: but as soon as John understood he went very red, and wanted to escape. The rest of
the children, on the other hand, were eaten with envy.

"Mayn't I help too?" piped Rachel.

The despairing mate thought he saw just a forlorn hope
in this. While John was being instructed, he gathered the
other children: and out of the heap of miscellaneous cloth-
ing rigged them all out in a sort of fancy dress. Then he
gave them the samples to carry round, and the sale began
anew.

It had now assumed rather the character of a parochial
bazaar. Even the Vicar was present—though less well
shaved than he would have been in England, and cun-
ninger-looking. He was one of the only buyers.

The children thoroughly enjoyed themselves, and
minced and pranced and tugged each other's turbans. But
the crowd was a Latin one, not Nordic: and their endear-
ing tricks failed altogether to arouse any interest. The sale
went worse than ever.

There was only one exception, and that was the important old lady. Once her attention had been called (by her

own act) to the children, it fixed itself on one of them, on Edward. She drew him to her bosom, like a mother in melodrama, and with her hairy mouth gave him three resounding kisses.

Edward could no more have struggled than if caught by a boa. Moreover, the portentous woman fascinated him, as if she had been a boa indeed. He lay in her arms limp, self-conscious, and dejected: but without active thought of escape.

And so the business went on: on the one hand the unheeded drone of the mate, on the other the great creature still keeping up her witticisms, still dominating everything: all of a sudden remembering Edward, and giving him a couple of kisses like so many bombs: then forgetting clean all about him: then remembering him again, and hugging him: then dropping her salts: then nearly dropping Edward: then suddenly twisting round to launch a dart into the crowd behind her—she was the despair of that unhappy auctioneer, who saw lot after lot fall for a tenth of its value, or even find no bidder at all.

Captain Jonsen, however, had his own idea of how to enliven a parochial bazaar that is proving a frost. He went on board, and mixed several gallons of that potion known in alcoholic circles as Hangman's Blood (which is compounded of rum, gin, brandy, and porter). Innocent (merely beery) as it looks, refreshing as it tastes, it has the property of increasing rather than allaying thirst, and so, once it has made a breach, soon demolishes the whole fort.

This he poured out into mugs, merely remarking that it was a noted English cordial, and gave it to the children to distribute among the crowd.

At once the Cubans began to show more interest in

them than when they came bearing samples of arrowroot; and with their popularity their happiness increased, and like rococo Ganymedekins and Hebelettes they darted about the crowd, distributing the enticing poison to all who would.

When he saw what was afoot, the mate wiped his mouth in despair.

"*Oh* you fool!" he groaned.

But the captain himself was highly pleased with his ruse: kept rubbing his hands, and grinning, and winking.

"That'll liven 'em, eh?"

"Wait and see!" was all the mate let himself say. "You just wait and see!"

"Look at Edward!" said Emily to Margaret in a pause. "It's perfectly sickening!"

It was. The very first mug rendered the fat señora even more motherly. Edward by now was fascinated, was in her power completely. He sat and gazed up in her little black eyes, his own large brown ones glazed with sentiment. He avoided her moustache, it is true: but on her cheek he was returning her kisses earnestly. All this, of course, without the possibility of their exchanging a single word—pure instinct. "With a fork drive Nature out . . ." One would gladly have taken a fork to Nature on that occasion.

Meanwhile, on the rest of the crowd the liquor was having exactly the effect the mate had foreseen. Instead of stimulating them, it dissolved completely whatever vestiges of attention they were still giving to the sale. He stepped down from the platform—gave it all up in despair. For they had now broken up into little groups, which discussed and argued their own affairs as if they were in a café. He in his turn went on board, and shut himself in his cabin—Captain Jonsen could deal with the mess he had made himself!

But alas! No worse host than Jonsen was ever born: he was utterly incapable of either understanding or controlling a crowd. All he could think of to do was to ply them with more.

For the children, the spectacle was an absorbing one. The whole nature of these people, as they drank, seemed to be changing: under their very eyes something seemed to be breaking up, like ice melting. Remember that to them this was a pantomime: no word spoken to explain, and so the eyes exercised a peculiar clearness.

It was rather as if the whole crowd had been immersed in water, and something dissolved out of them while the general structure yet remained) The tone of their voices changed, and they began to talk much slower, to move more slowly and elaborately. The expression of their faces became more candid, and yet more mask-like: hiding less, there was also less to hide. Two men even began to fight: but they fought so incompetently it was like a fight in a poetic play. Conversation, which before had a beginning and an end, now grew shapeless and interminable, and the women laughed a lot.

One old gentleman in most respectable clothes settled himself on the dirty ground at full length, with his head in the shade of the throned lady, spread a handkerchief over his face, and went to sleep; three other middle-aged men, holding each other with one hand to establish contact and using the other for emphasis, kept up a continuous clacking talk, that faltered intolerably though never quite stopping—like a very old engine.

A dog ran in and out among them all wagging its tail, but no one kicked it. Presently it found the old gentleman who was asleep on the ground, and began licking his ear excitedly: it had never had such a chance before.

The old lady also had fallen asleep, a little crookedly— she might even have slipped off her chair if her Negro had not buttressed her up. Edward got off her, and went and joined the other children rather shamefacedly: but they would not speak to him.

Jonsen looked round him perplexedly. Why had Otto abandoned the sale, now the crowd were all primed and ready? Probably he had some good reason, though. He was an incomprehensible man, that mate, but clever.

The truth is that Captain Jonsen was himself a man with a very weak head for liquor, and so he very seldom touched it, and knew little of the subtler aspects of its effects.

He paced up and down the dusty wharf at his usual slow shuffle, his head sunk forward in wretchedness, occasionally wringing his hands in the naturalest way, and even whimpering. When the priest came up to him confidentially and offered him a price for all that remained unsold he simply shook his head and continued his shuffle.

There was something a little nightmarelike in the whole scene which riveted the children's attention, and was very near the border of frightening them. It was with something of a struggle that at last Margaret said "Let's go on the ship." So they all went on board; and feeling a little unprotected even there descended into the hold, which was the safest place because they had already slept in it. They sat down on the kelson without doing or saying much, still with a vague apprehension, till boredom at last eliminated it.

"Oh I *wish* I had brought my paint-box!" said Emily, with a sigh fetched right up from her boots.

2

That night, after they had all gone to bed, they saw in a half-asleep state a lantern bobbing up and down in the open hatch. It was held by José, the little monkeyfied one (they had already decided he was the nicest of the crew). He was grinning winningly, and beckoning to them.

Emily was too sleepy to move, and so were Laura and Rachel; so, leaving them to lie, the others—Margaret, Edward and John—scrambled on deck.

It was mysteriously quiet. Not a sign of the crew, but for José. In the bright starlight the town looked abnormally beautiful: there was music coming from one of the big houses up by the church. José conducted them ashore and up to this house; tiptoed up to the jalousies and signed to them to follow him.

As the light struck his face it became transfigured, so affected was he by the opulence within.

The children craned up to the level of the windows and peered in too, oblivious of the mosquitoes making havoc of their necks.

It was a very grand sight. This was the house of the Chief Magistrate: and he was giving a dinner in honour of Captain Jonsen and his mate. There he sat at the head of the table, in uniform; very stiff, yet his little beard even stiffer than himself. His was the kind of dignity that grows from reserve and stillness, from freezing every minute like game which scents the hunter; while in total contrast to him there sat his wife (the important señora who had made so much of Edward), more impressive easily than her husband, but doing it not by dignity but by that calculated abandon and vulgarity which transcend dignity. Indeed, her flinging about got the greater part of its effect from the very formality of her setting.

When the children arrived at the window she must even have been discussing the size of her own belly: for she suddenly seized the shy hand of the mate, and made him, willy-nilly, feel it, as if to clench an argument.

As for her husband, he did not seem to see her: nor did the servants: she was such a very great lady.

But it was not her, it was the meal which raped José's attention. It was certainly an impressive one. Together on the table were tomato soup, mountain mullet, cray-fish, a huge red-snapper, land-crabs, rice and fried chicken, a young turkey, a small joint of goat-mutton, a wild duck, beefsteak, fried pork, a dish of wild pigeons, sweet potatoes, yuca, wine, and guavas and cream. It was a meal which would take a long time.

Captain Jonsen and the lady appeared to be on excellent terms: he pressing some project on her, and she, without the least loss of amiability, putting it on one side. What they were talking about, of course, the children could not hear. As a matter of fact, it was themselves. Captain Jonsen was trying to get the lady to discuss the disposal of his impromptu nursery: the most reasonable solution being plainly to leave them at Santa Lucia, more or less in her charge. But she was adept at eluding the importunate. It was not till the banquet was over that he realised he had failed to make any arrangement whatever.

But long before this, before the dinner was ended and the dance began, the children were tired of the peep-show. So José tiptoed away with them, down to the back streets by the dock. Presently they came to a mysterious door at the bottom of a staircase, with a Negro standing as if on guard. But he made no effort to stop them, and, José leading them, they climbed several flights to a large upper room.

The air was one you could hardly push through. The place was crowded with Negroes, and a few rather smudgy whites: among whom they recognised most of the rest of the crew of the schooner. At the far end was the most primitive stage you ever saw: there was a cradle on it, and a large star swung on the end of a piece of string. There was to be a Nativity-play—rather early in the season. While the Chief Magistrate entertained the pirate captain and mate, the priest had got this up in honour of the pirate crew.

A Nativity-play, with real cattle.

The whole audience had arrived an hour early, so as to see the entry of the cow. The children were just in time for this.

The room was in the upper part of a warehouse, which had been built, through some freak of vanity, in the English fashion, several stories high; and was provided with the usual large door opening onto nothingness, with a beam-and-tackle over it. Many the load of gold-dust and arrow-root which must have once been hoisted into it: now, like most of the others at Santa Lucia, it had long since ceased to be used.

But today a new rope had been rove through the block, and a broad belly-band put round the waist of the priest's protesting old cow.

Margaret and Edward lingered timidly near the top of the stairs; but John, putting his head down and burrowing like a mole, was not content till he had reached the open doorway. There he stood looking out into the darkness, where he saw a slowly revolving cow treading the air a yard from the sill, while at each revolution a Negro reached out to the utmost limit of balance, trying to catch her by the tail and draw her to shore.

John, in his excitement, leant out too far. He lost his balance and fell clear to the ground, forty feet, right on his head.

José gave a cry of alarm, sprang onto the cow's back, and was instantly lowered away—just as if the cinema had already been invented. He must have looked very comic. But what was going on inside him the while it is difficult to know. Such a responsibility does not often fall on an old sailor; and he would probably feel it all the more for that reason. As for the crowd beneath, they made no attempt to touch the body till José had completed his descent; they stood back and let him have a good look at it, and shake it, and so on. But the neck was quite plainly broken.

Margaret and Edward, however, had not any clear idea of what was going on, since they had not actually seen John fall. So they were rather annoyed when two of the schooner's crew appeared and insisted on their coming back to bed at once. They wanted to know where John was: but even more they wanted to know where José was, and why they weren't to be allowed to stay. However, they obeyed, in the impossibility of asking questions, and started back to bed.

Just as they were about to go on board the schooner, they heard a huge report on their left, like a cannon. They turned; and looking past the quiet, silver town, with its palm groves, to the hills behind, they saw a large ball of fire, travelling at a tremendous rate. It was quite close to the ground, and not very far off either—just beyond the church. It left a wake of the most brilliant blue, green, and purple blobs of light. For a while it hovered: then it burst, and the air was shortly charged with a strong sulphurous smell.

They were all frightened by the meteor, the sailors even more than the children, and hastened on board.

In the small hours, Edward suddenly called Emily in his sleep.

She woke up: "What is it?"

"It's rather cow-catching, isn't it?" he asked anxiously, his eyes tight shut.

"What's the matter?"

He did not answer, so she roused him—or thought she had.

"I only wanted to see if you were a *real* Cow-catching Zomfanelia," he explained in a kind voice: and was immediately deep asleep again.

In the morning they might easily have thought the whole thing a dream, if John's bed had not been so puzzlingly empty.

Yet, as if by some mute flash of understanding, no one commented on his absence. No one questioned Margaret, and she offered no information. Neither then nor thereafter was his name ever mentioned by anybody: and if you had known the children intimately you would never have guessed from them that he had ever existed.

3

The children's only enemy on board the schooner (which presently put to sea again, with them still on board) was the big white pig. (There was a little black fellow, too.)

He was a pig with no decision of mind. He could never choose a place to lie for himself, but was so ready to follow anyone else's opinion that whatever position you took up he immediately recognized as the best, the only site: and came and routed you out of it. Seeing how rare shady patches of deck are in a calm, or dry patches in a stiff breeze, this was a most infernal nuisance. One is so defenceless against big pigs when lying on one's back.

The little black one could be a nuisance also, it is true, but that was only from excess of friendliness. He hated to be left out of any party; nay more, he hated lying on inanimate matter, if a living couch was to be found.

On the north beach of Cape San Antonio it is possible to land a boat, if you pick your spot. About fifty yards through the bushes there are a couple of acres of open ground: cross this, and among some sharp coral rocks in the scrub on the far side are two wells, the northernmost the better of the two.

So, being becalmed off the Mangrove Keys one morning, Jonsen sent a boat on shore to get water.

The heat was extreme. The ropes hung like dead snakes, the sails as heavy as ill-sculptured drapery. The iron stanchion of the awning blistered any hand that touched it. Where the deck was unsheltered, the pitch boiled out of the seams. The children lay gasping together in the small shade, the little black pig squealing anxiously till he found a comfortable stomach to settle down on.

The big white pig had not found them yet.

From the silent shore came an occasional gun-shot. The water-party were potting pigeons. The sea was like a smooth pampas of quick-silver: so steady you could not split shore from reflection, till the casual collision of a pelican broke the phantom. The crew were mending sails, under the awning, with infinite slowness: all except one Negro, who straddled the bowsprit in his trousers, admiring his own grin in the mirror beneath. The sun lit an iridescent glimmer on his shoulders: in such a light even a

Negro could not be black.

Emily was missing John badly, but the little black pig snuffled in supreme content, his snout buried amicably in her arm-pit.

When the boatload returned, they had other game besides pigeons and grey land-crabs. They had stolen a goat from some lonely fisherman.

It was just as they came up over the side that the big white pig discovered the party under the awning, and prepared for the attack. But the goat at that moment bounded nimbly from the bulwarks, and without even stopping to look round, swallowed his chin and charged. He caught the old pig full in the ribs, knocking his wind out completely.

Then the battle began. The goat charged, the pig screamed and hustled. Each time the goat arrived at him the pig yelled as if he was killed; but each time the goat drew back the pig advanced towards him. The goat, his beard flying like a prophet's, his eyes crimson and his scut as lively as a lamb's at the teat, bounded in, bounded back into the bows for a fresh run: but at each charge his run grew shorter and shorter. The pig was hemming him in.

Suddenly the pig gave a frightful squeal, chiefly in surprise at his own temerity, and pounced. He had got the goat cornered against the windlass; and for a few flashing seconds bit and trampled.

It was a very chastened goat which was presently led off to his quarters: but the children were prepared to love him forever, for the heroic bangs he had given the old tyrant.

But he was not entirely inhuman, that pig. That same afternoon, he was lying on the hatch eating a banana. The ship's monkey was swinging on a loose tail of rope; and spotting the prize, swung further and further till at last he was able to snatch it from between the pig's very trotters. You would never have thought that the immobile mask of a pig could wear a look of such astonishment, such dismay, such piteous injury.

CHAPTER FIVE

When Destiny knocks the first nail in the coffin of a tyrant, it is seldom long before she knocks the last.

It was the very next morning that the schooner, in the lightest of airs, was sidling gently to leeward. The mate was at the wheel, shifting his weight from foot to foot with that rhythmic motion many steersmen affect, the better to get the feel of a finicky helm; and Edward was teaching the captain's terrier to beg, on the cabin-top. The mate shouted to him to hang on to something.

"Why?" said Edward.

"*Hang on!*" cried the mate again, spinning the wheel over as fast as he could to bring her into the wind.

The howling squall took her, through his promptness, almost straight in the nose; or it would have carried all away. Edward clung to the skylight. The terrier skidded about alarmedly all over the cabin-top, slipped off onto the deck, and was kicked by a dashing sailor clean through the galley door. But not so that poor big pig, who was taking an airing on deck at the time. Overboard he went, and vanished to windward, his snout (sometimes) sticking up manfully out of the water. God, Who had sent him the goat and the monkey for a sign, now required his soul of him. Overboard, too, went the coops of fowls, three new-washed shirts, and—of all strange things to get washed away—the grindstone.

Up out of his cabin appeared the captain's shapeless brown head, cursing the mate as if it was *he* who had upset the apple-cart. He came up without his boots, in grey wool socks, and his braces hanging down his back.

"Get below!" muttered the mate furiously: "I can manage her!"

The captain did not, however: still in his socks he came up on deck and took the wheel out of the mate's hand. The latter went a dull brick-red, walked for'ard, then aft again, then went below and shut himself in his cabin.

In a few moments the wind had combed up some quite hearty waves: then it blew their tops off, and so flattened the sea out again, a sea that was black except for little whipt-up fountains of iridescent foam.

"Get my boots!" bellowed Jonsen at Edward.

Edward dashed down the companion with alacrity. It is a great moment, one's first order at sea; especially when it comes in an emergency. He re-appeared with a boot in each hand, and a lurch flung him boots and all at the captain's feet.

"Never carry things in both hands," said the captain, smiling pleasantly.

"Why?" asked Edward.

"Keep one hand to lay hold with."

There was a pause.

"Someday, I will teach you the Three Sovereign Rules of Life." He shook his head meditatively. "They are very wise. But not yet. You are too young."

"Why not?" asked Edward: "When shall I be old enough?"

The captain considered, going over the Rules in his head.

"When you know which is windward and which is lee-ward, then I will teach you the first rule."

Edward made his way forward, determined to qualify as soon as he possibly could.

When the worst of the squall was over they got the advantage of it, the schooner lying over lissomly and spinning along like a race-horse. The crew were in great spirits—chaffing the carpenter, who, they declared, had thrown his grindstone overboard as a life-buoy for the pig.

The children were in good spirits also. Their shyness was all gone now. The schooner lying over as she did, her wet deck made a most admirable toboggan-slide; and for half an hour they tobogganed happily on their bottoms from windward to leeward, shrieking with joy, fetching up in the lee scuppers, which were mostly awash, and then climbing from thing to thing to the windward bul-warks raised high in the air, and so all over again.

Throughout that half hour, Jonsen at the wheel said not a single word. But at last his pent-up irritation broke out:

"Hi! You! Stop that!"

They gazed at him in astonishment and disillusion.

There is a period in the relations of children with any new grown-up in charge of them, the period between first acquaintance and the first reproof, which can only be compared to the primordial innocence of Eden. Once a reproof has been administered, this can never be recov-ered again.

Jonsen now had done it.

But he was not content with that—he was still bursting with rage:

"Stop it! Stop it, I tell you!"

(They had already done so, of course.)

The whole unreasonableness, the monstrousness of the imposition of these brats on his ship suddenly came over him, and summed itself up in a single symbol:

"If you go and wear holes in your drawers, do you think *I* am going to mend them? Lieber Gott! What do you think I am, eh? What do you think this ship is? What do you think we all are? To mend your drawers for you, eh? *To mend . . . your . . . drawers?*"

There was a pause, while they all stood thunderstruck.

But even now he had not finished:

"Where do you think you'll get new ones, eh?" he asked, in a voice explosive with rage. Then he added, with an insulting coarseness of tone: "And I'll not have you going about my ship without them! See?"

Scarlet to the eyes with outrage they retreated to the bows. They could hardly believe so unspeakable a remark had crossed human lips. They assumed an air of lightness, and talked together in studied loud voices: but their joy was dashed for the day.

So it was that—small as a man's hand—a spectre began to show over their horizon: the suspicion at last that this was *not* all according to plan, that they might even be not wanted. For a while their actions showed the unhappy wariness of the uninvited guest.

Later in the afternoon, Jonsen, who had not spoken again, but looked from time to time acutely miserable, was still at the wheel. The mate had shaved himself and put on shore clothes, as a parable: he now appeared on deck, pretended not to see the captain, but strolled like a passenger up to the children and entered into conversation with them.

"If I'm not fit to steer in foul weather, I'm not fit to steer in fair!" he muttered, but without glancing at the captain. "He can take the helum all day and night, for all the help *I'll* give him!"

The captain appeared equally not to see the mate. He looked quite ready to take both watches till kingdom come.

"If *he'd* been at the wheel when that squall struck us," said the mate under his voice but with biting passion, "he'd have lost the ship! He's no more eye for a squall coming than a sucker-fish! And he knows it, too: that's what makes him go on this way!"

The children did not answer. It shocked them deeply to have to see a grown-up, a should-be Olympian, displaying his feelings. In exact oppositon to the witnesses at the Transfiguration, they felt it would have been good for them to be almost anywhere rather than there. He was totally unconscious of their discomfort, however: too self-occupied to notice how they avoided catching his eye.

"Look! There's a steamship!" exclaimed Margaret, with much too bright a brightness.

The mate glowered at it.

"Aye, they'll be the death of us, those steamers," he said. "Every year there's more of them. They'll be using them for men-of-war next, and then where'll we be? Times are bad enough without steamers."

But while he spoke he wore a preoccupied expression, as if he were more concerned with what was going on at the back of his mind than with what went on in the front.

"Did you ever hear about what happened when the first steamer put to sea in the Gulf of Paria?" he asked, however.

"No, what?" asked Margaret, with an eagerness that even exceeded the necessities of politeness in its falsity.

"She was built on the Clyde, and sailed over. (Nobody

thought of using steam for a long ocean voyage in those days.) The Company thought they ought to make a to-do—to popularise her, so to speak. So the first time she put to sea under her own power, they invited all the big-wigs on board: all the Members of Assembly in Trinidad, and the Governor and his staff, and a Bishop. It was the Bishop what did the trick."

His story died out: he became completely absorbed in watching sidelong the effect of his bravado on the captain.

"Did what?" asked Margaret.

"Ran 'em aground."

"But what did they let him steer for?" asked Edward: "They might have known he couldn't!"

"Edward! How dare you talk about a Bishop in that rude way!" admonished Rachel.

"It wasn't the steamer he run aground, sonny," said the mate. "It was a poor innocent little devil of a pirate craft, that was just beating up for the Boca Grande in a northerly breeze."

"Good for him!" said Edward. "How did he do it?"

"They were all sea-sick, being on a steamer for the first time: the way she rolls, not like a decent sailing vessel. There wasn't a man who could stay on deck—except the Bishop, and he just thrived on it. So when the poor little pirate cut under her bows, and seen her coming up in the eye of the wind, no sail set, with a cloud of smoke amidships and an old Bishop bung in the middle of the smoke, and her paddles making as much turmoil as a whale trying to scratch a flea in its ear, he just beached his vessel and took to the woods. Never went to sea again, he didn't: started growing coconuts. But there was one poor fish was in such a hurry he broke his leg, and they came

ashore and found him. When he saw the Bishop coming
for him he started yelling out it was the Devil."

"O-oh!" gasped Rachel, horror-struck.

"How silly of him," said Edward.

"I don't know so much!" said the mate. "He wasn't too
far wrong! Ever since that, they've been the death of our
profession, Steam and the Church . . . what with steaming, and what with preaching, and steaming and preaching. . . . Now that's a funny thing," he broke off, suddenly
interested by what he was saying: "*Steam* and the
Church! What have they got in common, eh? Nothing,
you'd say. You'd think they'd fight each other cat-and-
dog; but no, they're thick as two thieves . . . thick as
thieves. —Not like in the days of Parson Audain."

"Who was he?" asked Margaret helpfully.

"He was a right sort of a parson, he was, *yn wyr iawn!*
He was Rector of Roseau—oh, a long time back."

"Here! Come and take this wheel while I have a spell!"
grunted the captain.

"I couldn't well say *how* long back," continued the mate
in a loud, unnatural, and now slightly exultant voice:
"Forty years or more."

He began to tell the story of the famous Rector of
Roseau: one of the finest pathetic preachers of his age,
according to contemporaries; whose appearance was fine,
gentle, and venerable, and who supplemented his stipend
by owning a small privateer.

"Here! Otto!" called Jonsen.

But the mate had a long recital of the parson's misfor-
tunes before him: beginning with the capture of his
schooner (while smuggling Negroes to Guadaloupe), by
another privateer, from Nevis; and how the parson went
to Nevis, posted his rival's name on the courthouse door,

and stood on guard there with loaded pistols for three days in the hope the man would come and challenge him.

"What, to fight a *duel?*" asked Harry.

"But wasn't he a clergyman, you said?" asked Emily.

But duels, it appeared, did not come amiss to this priest. He fought thirteen altogether in his life, the mate told them: and on one occasion, while waiting for the seconds to reload, he went up to his opponent, suggested "just a little something to fill in time, good sir," —and knocked him flat with his fist.

This time, however, his enemy lay low: so he fitted out a second schooner, and took command of her, weekdays, himself. His first quarry was an apparently harmless Spanish merchantman: but she suddenly opened fourteen masked gun-ports and it was he who had to surrender. All his crew were massacred but himself and his carpenter, who hid behind a water-cask all night."

"But I don't understand," said Margaret. "Was he a pirate?"

"Of course he was!" said Otto the mate.

"Then *why* did you say he was a clergyman?" pursued Emily.

The mate looked as puzzled as she did. "Well, he was Rector of Roseau, wasn't he? And B.A., B.D.?—Anyway, he was rector until the new Governor listened to some cock-and-bull story against him, and made him resign. He was the best preacher they ever had—he'd have been a bishop one day, if someone hadn't slandered him to the Governor!"

"Otto!" called the captain in a conciliatory voice. "Come over here, I want to speak to you."

But the deaf and exulting mate had plenty of his story still to run: how Audain now turned trader, and took a cargo of corn to San Domingo, and settled there: how he challenged two black generals to a duel, and shot them both, and Christophe threatened to hang him if they died. But the parson (having little faith in Domingan doctors) escaped by night in an open boat and went to St. Eustatius. There he found many religions but no ministers; so he recommenced clergyman of every kind: in the morning he celebrated a mass for the Catholics, then a Lutheran service in Dutch, then Church of England matins: in the evening he sang hymns and preached hell-fire to the Methodists. Meanwhile his wife, who had more tranquil tastes, lived at Bristol; so he now married a Dutch widow, resourcefully conducting the ceremony himself.

"But I *don't* understand!" said Emily despairingly: "Was he a real clergyman?"

"Of course he wasn't," said Margaret.

"But he couldn't have married himself *himself* if he wasn't," argued Edward: "Could he?"

The mate heaved a sigh.

"But the English Church aren't like that nowadays," he said: "They're all against us."

"I should think not, indeed!" pronounced Rachel slowly, in a deep indignant voice. "He was a very wicked man!"

"He was a most respectable person," replied the mate severely, "and a *wonderful* pathetic preacher!—You may take it they were chagrined at Roseau when they heard St. Eustatius had got him!"

Captain Jonsen had lashed the wheel, and came up, his face piteous with distress.

"Otto! Mein Schatz . . . !" he began, laying his great bear's-arm round the mate's neck. Without more ado they went below together, and a sailor came aft unbidden and took the wheel.

Ten minutes later the mate reappeared on deck for a moment, and sought out the children.

"What's the captain been saying to you?" he asked. "Flashed out at you about something, did he?"

He took their complex, uncomfortable silence for assent.

"Don't you take too much notice of what he says," he went on. "He flashes out like that sometimes; but a minute after he could eat himself, fair eat himself!"

The children stared at him in astonishment: what on earth was he trying to say?

But he seemed to think he had explained his mission fully: turned, and once more went below.

For hours a merry but rather tedious hubble-bubble, suggesting liquor, was heard ascending from the cabin skylight. As evening drew on, the breeze having dropped away almost to a calm, the steersman reported that both Jonsen and Otto were now fast asleep, their heads on each other's shoulders across the cabin table. As he had long forgotten what the course was, but had been simply steering by the wind, and there was now no wind to steer by, he (the steersman) concluded the wheel could get on very well without him.

The reconciliation of the captain and the mate deserved to be celebrated by all hands with a blind.

A rum cask was broached; and the common sailors were soon as unconscious as their betters.

Altogether this was one of the unpleasantest days the children had spent in their lives.

When dawn came, everyone was still pretty incapable, and the neglected vessel drooped uncertainly. Jonsen, still rather unsteady on his feet, his head aching and his mind

Napoleonic but muddled, came on deck and looked about him. The sun had come up like a searchlight; but it was about all there was to be seen. No land was anywhere in sight, and the sea and sky seemed very uncertain as to the most becoming place to locate their mutual firmament. It was not till he had looked round and round a fair number of times that he perceived a vessel, up in what by all appearances must be sky, yet not very far distant.

For some little while he could not remember what it is a pirate captain does when he sees a sail, and he felt in no mood to overtax his brain by trying to. But after a time it came back unbidden—one gives chase.

"Give chase!" he ordered solemnly to the morning air; and then went below again and roused the mate, who roused the crew.

No one had the least idea where they were, or what kind of a craft this quarry might be; but such considerations were altogether too complicated for the moment. As the sun parted farther from his reflection a breeze sprung up; so the sails were trimmed after a fashion, and chase was duly given. In an hour or two, as the air grew clearer, it was plain their quarry was a merchant brig, not too heavily laden and making a fair pace: a pace, indeed, which in their incompetently trimmed condition they were finding it pretty difficult to equal. Jonsen shuffled rapidly up and down the deck like a shuttle, passing his woof backwards and forwards through the real business of the ship. He was hugging himself with excitement, trying to evolve some crafty scheme of capture. The chase went on: but noon past, the distance between the two vessels was barely, if at all, lessened. Jonsen, however, was much too optimistic to realise this.

It used to be a common device of pirates when in chase

of a vessel to tow behind them a spare topmast, or some other bulky object. This would act as a drogue, or brake: and the pursued, seeing them with all sail set apparently doing their utmost, would underestimate their powers of speed. Then when night fell the pirate would haul the spar on board, overtake the other vessel rapidly and catch it unprepared.

There were several reasons why this device was unsuitable to the present occasion. First and most obviously, it was doubtful whether, in their present condition, they were capable of overtaking the brig at all, leaving such handicaps altogether out of consideration. A second was that the brig showed no signs of alarm. She was proceeding on her voyage at her natural pace, quite unaware of the honour they were doing her.

However, Captain Jonsen was nothing if not a crafty man; and during the afternoon he gave orders for a spare spar to be towed behind as I have described. The result was that the schooner lost ground rapidly: and when night fell they were at least a couple of miles further from the brig than they had been at dawn. When night fell, of course, they hauled the spar on board and prepared for the last act. They followed the brig by compass through the hours of darkness, without catching sight of her. When morning came, all hands crowded expectantly at the rail.

But the brig was vanished. The sea was as bare as an egg.

If they were lost before, now they were double-lost. Jonsen did not know where he might be within two hundred miles; and being no sextant-man, but an incurable dead-reckoner, he had no means of finding out. This did not worry him very greatly, however, because sooner or

later one of two things might happen: he might catch
sight of some bit of land he recognised, or he might capture some vessel better informed than himself. Meanwhile, since he had no particular destination, one bit of
sea was much the same to him as another.

The piece he was wandering in, however, was evidently
out of the main track of shipping; for days went by, and
weeks, without his coming even so near to effecting a capture as he had been in the case of the brig.

But Captain Jonsen was not sorry to be out of the public eye for a while. Before he had left Santa Lucia, news
had reached him of the *Clorinda* putting in to Havana;
and of the fantastic tale Marpole was telling. The "twelve
disguised gunports" had amused him hugely, since he was
altogether without artillery; but when he heard Marpole
accused him of murdering the children—Marpole, that
least reputable of skunks—his anger had broken out in
one of its sudden explosions. For it was unthinkable—
during those first few days—that he would ever touch a
hair of their heads, or even speak a cross word to them.
They were still a sort of holy novelty, then; it was not till
their shyness had worn off that he had begun to regret so
whole-heartedly the failure of his attempt to leave them
behind with the Chief Magistrate's wife.

CHAPTER SIX

The weeks passed in aimless wandering. For the children, the lapse of time acquired once more the texture of a dream: things ceased happening: every inch of the schooner was now as familiar to them as the *Clorinda* had been, or Ferndale: they settled down quietly to grow, as they had done at Ferndale, and as they would have done, had there been time, on the *Clorinda*.

And then an event did occur, to Emily, of considerable importance. She suddenly realised who she was.

There is little reason that one can see why it should not have happened to her five years earlier, or even five later; and none why it should have come that particular afternoon.

She had been playing houses in a nook right in the bows, behind the windlass (on which she had hung a devil's-claw as a doorknocker); and tiring of it was walking rather aimlessly aft, thinking vaguely about some bees and a fairy queen, when it suddenly flashed into her mind that she was *she*.

She stopped dead, and began looking over all of her person which came within the range of her eyes. She could not see much, except a fore-shortened view of the front of her frock, and her hands when she lifted them for inspection; but it was enough for her to form a rough idea of the little body she suddenly realised to be hers.

She began to laugh, rather mockingly. "Well!" she thought, in effect: "Fancy *you*, of all people, going and getting caught like this!—You can't get out of it now, not for a very long time: you'll have to go through with being a child, and growing up, and getting old, before you'll be quit of this mad prank!"

Determined to avoid any interruption of this highly important occasion, she began to climb the ratlines, on her way to her favourite perch at the masthead. Each time she moved an arm or a leg in this simple action, however, it struck her with fresh amazement to find them obeying her so readily. Memory told her, of course, that they had always done so before: but before, she had never realised how surprising this was.

Once settled on her perch, she began examining the skin of her hands with the utmost care: for it was *hers*. She slipped a shoulder out of the top of her frock; and having peeped in to make sure she really was continuous under her clothes, she shrugged it up to touch her cheek. The contact of her face and the warm bare hollow of her shoulder gave her a comfortable thrill, as if it was the caress of some kind friend. But whether the feeling came to her through her cheek or her shoulder, which was the caresser and which the caressed, that no analysis could tell her.

Once fully convinced of this astonishing fact, that she was now Emily Bas-Thornton (why she inserted the "now" she did not know, for she certainly imagined no transmigrational nonsense of having been anyone else before), she began seriously to reckon its implications.

First, what agency had so ordered it that out of all the people in the world who she might have been, she was this particular one, this Emily; born in such-and-such a year out of all the years in Time, and encased in this particular rather pleasing little casket of flesh? Had she chosen herself, or had God done it?

At this, another consideration: who was God? She had heard a terrible lot about Him, always: but the question of His identity had been left vague, as much taken for granted as her own. Wasn't she perhaps God herself? Was it that she was trying to remember? However, the more she tried, the more it eluded her. (How absurd, to disremember such an important point as whether one was God or not!) So she let it slide: perhaps it would come back to her later.

Secondly, why had all this not occurred to her before? She had been alive for over ten years, now, and it had never once entered her head. She felt like a man who suddenly remembers at eleven o'clock at night, sitting in his own arm-chair, that he had accepted an invitation to go out to dinner that night. There is no reason for him to remember it now: but there seems equally little why he should not have remembered it in time to keep his engagement. How could he have sat there all the evening without being disturbed by the slightest misgiving? How could Emily have gone on being Emily for ten years without once noticing this apparently obvious fact?

It must not be supposed that she argued it all out in this ordered but rather long-winded fashion. Each consideration came to her in a momentary flash, quite innocent of

words; and in between her mind lazed along, either thinking of nothing or returning to her bees and the fairy queen.
If one added up the total of her periods of conscious
thought, it would probably reach something between four
and five seconds; nearer five, perhaps; but it was spread
out over the best part of an hour.

Well then, granted she was Emily, what were the consequences, besides enclosure in that particular little body
(which now began on its own account to be aware of a
sort of unlocated itch, most probably somewhere on the
right thigh), and lodgement behind a particular pair of
eyes?

It implied a whole series of circumstances. In the first
place, there was her family, a number of brothers and
sisters from whom, before, she had never entirely dis-
sociated herself; but now she got such a sudden feeling of
being a discrete person that they seemed as separate from
her as the ship itself. However, willy-nilly she was almost
as tied to them as she was to her body. And then there
was this voyage, this ship, this mast round which she had
wound her legs. She began to examine it with almost as
vivid an illumination as she had studied the skin of her
hands. And when she came down from the mast, what
would she find at the bottom? There would be Jonsen, and
Otto, and the crew, the whole fabric of a daily life which
up to now she had accepted as it came, but which now
seemed vaguely disquieting. What was going to happen?
Were there disasters running about loose, disasters which
her rash marriage to the body of Emily Thornton made
her vulnerable to?

A sudden terror struck her: did anyone know? (Know,
I mean, that she was someone in particular, Emily—
perhaps even God—not just any little girl.) She could not

tell why, but the idea terrified her. It would be bad
enough if they should discover she was a particular
person—but if they should discover she was God! At all
costs she must hide *that* from them.—But suppose they
knew already, had simply been hiding it from her (as
guardians might from an infant king)? In that case, as in
the other, the only thing to do was to continue to behave
as if she did not know, and so outwit them.

But if she was God, why not turn all the sailors into
white mice, or strike Margaret blind, or cure somebody,
or do some other Godlike act of the kind? Why should she
hide it? She never really asked herself why: but instinct
prompted her strongly of the necessity. Of course, there
was the element of doubt (suppose she had made a mistake, and the miracle missed fire): but more largely it was
the feeling that she would be able to deal with the situation so much better when she was a little older. Once she
had declared herself, there would be no turning back; it
was much better to keep her godhead up her sleeve, for
the present.

Grown-ups embark on a life of deception with considerable misgiving, and generally fail. But not so children. A
child can hide the most appalling secret without the least
effort, and is practically secure against detection. Parents,
finding that they see through their child in so many places
the child does not know of, seldom realise that, if there is
some point the child really gives his mind to hiding, their
chances are nil.

So Emily had no misgivings when she determined to
preserve her secret, and needed have none.

Down below on the deck the smaller children were repeatedly crowding themselves into a huge coil of rope,
feigning sleep and then suddenly leaping out with yelps

of panic and dancing round it in consternation and dismay. Emily watched them with that impersonal attention one gives to a kaleidoscope. Presently Harry spied her, and gave a hail.

"Emilee-ee! Come down and play House-on-fire!"

At that, her normal interests momentarily revived. Her stomach as it were leaped within her sympathetically toward the game. But it died in her as suddenly: and not only died, but she did not even feel disposed to waste her noble voice on them. She continued to stare without making any reply whatever.

"Come on!" shouted Edward.

"Come and play!" shouted Laura. "Don't be a pig!"

Then in the ensuing stillness Rachel's voice floated up: "Don't call her, Laura, we don't really want her."

2

But Emily was completely unaffected—only glad that for the present they were all right by themselves. She was already beginning to feel the charge of the party a burden.

It had automatically devolved on her with the defection of Margaret.

It was puzzling, this Margaret business. She could not understand it, and it disturbed her. It dated back really to that night, about a week ago, when she herself had so unaccountably bitten the captain. The memory of her own extraordinary behaviour gave her now quite a little shiver of alarm.

Everybody had been very drunk that night, and making a terrible racket—it was impossible to get to sleep. So at last Edward had asked her to tell them a story. But she

was not feeling "storyable," so they had asked Margaret;
all except Rachel, who had begged Margaret not to, because she wanted to think, she said. But Margaret had
been very pleased at being asked, and had begun a very
stupid story about a princess who had lots and lots of
clothes and was always beating her servant for making
mistakes and shutting him up in a dark cupboard. The
whole story, really, had been nothing but clothes and
beating, and Rachel had *begged* her to stop.

In the middle, a sort of rabble of sailors had come down
the ladder, very slowly and with much discussion. They
stood at the bottom in a knot, swaying a little and all
turned inwards on one of their number. It was so dark one
could not see who it was. They were urging him to do
something—he hanging back.

"Oh, damn it!" he cried in a thick voice: "Bring me a
light, I can't see where dey are!"

It was the voice of the captain—but how altered! There
was a sort of suppressed excitement in it. Someone lit a
lantern and held it up in the middle. Captain Jonsen
stood on his legs half like a big sack of flour, half like a
waiting tiger.

"What do you want?" Emily had asked kindly.

But Captain Jonsen stood irresolute, shifting his weight
from foot to foot as if he was steering.

"You're drunk, aren't you?" Rachel had piped, loudly
and disapprovingly.

But it was Margaret who had behaved most queerly.
She had gone yellow as cheese, and her eyes large with
terror. She was shivering from head to foot as if she had
the fever. It was absurd. Then Emily remembered how
stupidly frightened Margaret had been the very first night
on the schooner.

At that moment Jonsen had staggered up to Emily, and putting one hand under her chin had begun to stroke her hair with the other. A sort of blind vertigo seized her: she caught his thumb and bit it as hard as she could, then, terrified at her own madness, dashed across the hold to where the other children were gathered in a wondering knot.

"What *have* you done!" cried Laura, pushing her away angrily: "Oh you wicked girl, you've hurt him!"

Jonsen was stamping about, swearing and sucking his thumb. Edward had produced a handkerchief, and between them all they had managed to tie it up. He stood staring at the bandaged member for a few moments; shook his head like a wet retriever and retreated on deck, dang-danging under his breath. Margaret had then been so ill they thought she must really have caught fever, and they couldn't get any sense out of her at all.

As Emily, with her new-found consciousness, recapitulated the scene, it was like rereading a story in a book, so little responsibility did she feel for the merely mechanical creature who had bitten the captain's thumb. Nor was she even very interested: it had been queer, but then there was very little in life which didn't seem queer now.

As for Jonsen, he and Emily had avoided each other ever since, by mutual consent. She indeed had been in Coventry with everybody for biting him; none of the other children would play with her all the next day, and she recognised that she thoroughly deserved it—it was a *mad* thing to have done. And yet Jonsen, in avoiding her, had himself more the air of being ashamed than angry . . . it was unaccountable.

But what interested her even more was the curious way Margaret had gone on, the next few days.

For some time she had behaved very oddly indeed. At first she seemed exaggeratedly frightened of all the men: but then she had suddenly taken to following them about the deck like a dog—not Jonsen, it is true, but Otto especially. Then suddenly she had departed from them altogether, and taken up her quarters in the cabin.

The curious thing was that now she avoided them all utterly, and spent all her time with the sailors: and the sailors, for their part, seemed to take peculiar pains not only not to let her speak to, but even not to let her be seen by, the other children.

Now they hardly saw her at all; and when they did she seemed so different they hardly recognised her: though where the difference lay it would be hard to say.

Emily, from her perch at the masthead, could just see the girl's head now, through the cabin skylight. Further forward, José had joined the children at their game, and was crawling about on hands and knees with all of them on his back—a fire-engine, of course, such as they had seen in the illustrated magazines from England.

"Emily!" called Harry: "Come and play!"

Down with a rush fell the curtain on all Emily's cogitations. In a second she was once more a happy little animal —*any* happy little animal. She slid down the shrouds like a real sailor, and in no time was directing the fire-fighting operations as imperiously as any other of this brigade of superintendents.

3

That night in the Parliament of Beds there was raised at last a question which you may well be surprised had not been raised before. Emily had just reduced her family to silence by sheer ferocity when Harry's rapid, nervous, lisping voice piped up:

"Emily, Emily, may I ask you a question please?"

"Go to sleep!"

There was a moment's whispered confabulation.

"But it's very important, please, and we all want to know."

"What?"

"Are these people pirates?"

Emily sat bold upright with astonishment.

"Of course not!"

Harry sounded rather crestfallen.

"I don't know. . . . I just thought they might. . . ."

"But they *are!*" declared Rachel firmly: "Margaret told me!"

"Nonsense!" said Emily: "There aren't any pirates nowadays."

"Margaret said," went on Rachel, "that time we were shut up on the other ship she heard one of the sailors calling out pirates had come on board."

Emily had an inspiration.

"No, you silly, he must have said *pilots.*"

"What are pilots?" asked Laura.

"They come on board," explained Emily, lamely. "Don't you remember that picture in the dining-room at home, called 'The Pilot Comes On Board'?"

Laura listened with rapt attention. The explanation of what pilots were was not very illuminating; but then she did not know what pirates were either. So you might think the whole discussion meant very little to her, but there you would be wrong: the question was evidently important to the older ones, therefore she gave her whole mind to listening.

The pirate heresy was considerably shaken. How could they say for certain which word Margaret had really heard? Rachel changed sides.

"They can't be pirates," she said: "Pirates are wicked."

"Couldn't we ask them?" Edward persisted.

Emily considered.

"I don't think it would be very polite."

"I'm sure they wouldn't mind," said Edward: "They're awfully decent."

"I think they mightn't like it," said Emily. In her heart she was afraid of the answer; and if they were pirates, it would here again be better to pretend not to know.

"I know!" she said: "Shall I ask the Mouse with the Elastic Tail?"

"Yes, do!" cried Laura. It was months since the oracle had been consulted; but her faith was still perfect.

Emily communed with herself in a series of short squeaks.

"He says they are *Pilots*," she announced.

"Oh," said Edward deeply: and they all went to sleep.

CHAPTER SEVEN

Edward often thought, as he strode scowling up and down the deck by himself, that this was exactly the life for him. What a lucky boy he was, to have tumbled into it by good fortune, instead of having to run away to sea as most other people did! In spite of the White Mouse's pronouncement (whom secretly he had long ceased to believe in), he had no doubt that this was a pirate vessel; and no doubt either that when presently Jonsen was killed in some furious battle the sailors would unanimously elect him their captain.

The girls were a great nuisance. A ship was no place for them. When he was captain he would have them marooned.

Yet there had been a time when he had wished he was a girl himself. "When I was young," he once confided to the admiring Harry, "I used to think girls were bigger and stronger than boys. Weren't I silly?"

"Yes," said Harry.

Harry did not confide it to Edward, but he also, *now*,

wished he was a girl. It was not for the same reason:
younger than Edward, he was still at the amorous age;
and because he found the company of girls almost mag-
ically pleasing, fondly imagined it would be even more so
if he were one himself. He was always finding himself, for
being a boy, shut out from their most secret councils.
Emily of course was too old to count as female in his eyes:
but to Rachel and Laura he was indiscriminately devoted.
When Edward was captain, he would be mate: and
when he imagined this future, it consisted for the most
part in rescuing Rachel—or Laura, *n'importe*—from new
and complicated dangers.

They were all by now just as much at home on the
schooner as they had been in Jamaica. Indeed, nothing
very continuous was left of Ferndale for the youngest
ones: only a number of luminous pictures of quite unim-
portant incidents. Emily of course remembered most
things, and could put them together. The death of Tabby,
for instance: she would never forget that as long as she
lived. She could recollect, too, that Ferndale had tumbled
down flat. And her Earthquake: she had been in an earthquake, and could remember every detail of *that*. Had it
been as a result of the earthquake that Ferndale had
tumbled down? That sounded likely. There had been
quite a high wind at that time, too. . . . She could remember that they had all been bathing when the earthquake
had come, and then had ridden somewhere on ponies. But
they had been *in* the house when it fell down: she was
pretty sure of that. It was all a little difficult to join up.—
Then when was it she had found that Negro village?
She could remember with a startling clearness bending
down, and feeling among the bamboo roots for the bubbling spring, then looking round and seeing the black

children scampering away up the clearing. That must
have been years and years ago. But clearer than everything was that awful night when Tabby had stalked up
and down the room, his eyes blazing and his fur twitching,
his voice melodious with tragedy, until those horrible
black shapes had flown in through the fanlight and sav-
aged him out into the bush. The horror of the scene was
even increased because it had once or twice come back to
her in dreams, and because when she dreamt it (though it
seemed the same) there was always some frightful difference. One night (and that was the worst of all) she had
rushed out to rescue him, when her darling faithful Tabby
had come up to her with the same horrible look on his
face the captain had worn that time she bit his thumb,
and had chased her down avenues and avenues and avenues and avenues of cabbage-palms, with Exeter House at
the end of them never getting any nearer however much
she ran. She knew, of course, it was not the real Tabby,
but a sort of diabolic double: and Margaret had sat up an
orange tree jeering at her, gone as black as a Negro.

One of the drawbacks of life at sea was the cockroaches. They were winged. They infested the hold, and
the smell they made was horrible. One had to put up with
them. But one didn't do much washing at sea; and it was
a common thing to wake up in the morning and find the
brutes had gnawed the quick from under one's nails, or
gnawed all the hard skin off the soles of one's feet, so that
one could hardly walk. Anything in the least greasy or
dirty they set on at once. Buttonholes were their especial
delight. One did little washing: fresh water was too valuable, and salt water had practically no effect. From han-
dling tarry ropes and greasy ironwork their hands would
have disgraced a slum child. There is a sailor saying which

includes a peck of dirt in the mariner's monthly rations: but the children on the schooner must have often consumed far more.

Not that it was a dirty ship—the fo'c'sle probably was, but the Nordicism of captain and mate kept the rest looking clean enough. But even the cleanest-looking ship is seldom clean to the touch. Their clothes José washed occasionally with his own shirt, and in that climate they were dry again by the morning.

Jamaica had faded into the past. England, to which they had supposed they were going, and of which a very curious picture had formerly been built up in their minds by their parents' constant reference to it, receded again into the mists of myth. They lived in the present, adapted themselves to it, and might have been born in a hammock and christened at a binnacle before they had been there many weeks. They seemed to have no natural fear of heights, and the farther they were above the deck, the happier. On a calm day Edward used to hang by his knees from the crosstrees in order to feel the blood run into his head. The flying-jib, too, which was usually down, made an admirable cocoon for hide-and-seek: one took a firm grip of the hanks and robands, and swathed oneself in the canvas. Once, suspecting Edward was hidden there, instead of going out on the jib-boom to look, the other children cast off the down-haul and then all together gave a great tug at the halyard which nearly pitched him into the sea. The shark myth is greatly exaggerated: it is untrue, for instance, that they can take a leg clean off at the hip—their bite is a tearing one, not a clean cut: and a practised bather can keep them off easily with a welt on the nose each time they turn over to strike:[1] but all the

[1] The tiger shark of the South Seas is of course a very different cattle.

same, once overboard there would have been little hope for a small boy like Edward; and a severe wigging they all got for their prank.

Often several of those thick, rubber-like protuberances would follow the vessel for hours—perhaps in the hope of just some such antic.

Sharks were not without their uses, however: it is well known that Catch a Shark Catch a Breeze, so when a breeze was needed the sailors baited a big hook and presently hauled one on board with the winch. The bigger he was, the better breeze was hoped for: and his tail was nailed to the jib-boom. One day they got a great whacking fellow on board, and having cut off his jaw someone heaved it into the ship's latrine (which no one was so lubberly as to use for its proper purpose), and thought no more about it. One wildish night, however, old José did go there, and sat full on that wicked cheval-de-frise. He yelled like a madman, and the crew were better pleased than they had been with any joke that year and even Emily thought if only it had been less improper how funny it would have been. It would certainly have puzzled an archæologist, faced with José's mummy, to guess how he came by those curious scars.

The ship's monkey also added a lot to the ship's merriment. One day some sucker-fish had fixed themselves firmly to the deck, and he undertook to dislodge them. After a few preliminary tugs, he braced three legs and his tail against the deck and lunged like a madman. But they would not budge. The crew were standing round in a ring, and he felt his honour was at stake: somehow, they *must* be removed. So, disgusting though they must have tasted to a vegetarian, he set to and ate them, right down to the sucker, and was loudly applauded.

Edward and Harry often talked over how they would distinguish themselves in the next engagement. Sometimes they would rehearse it: storm the galley with uncouth shouts, or spring into the main rigging and order everyone to be thrown into the sea. Once, as they went into battle,

"I am armed with a sword and a pistol!" chanted Edward:

"And I am armed with a key and a half a whist-le!" chanted the more literal Harry.

They took care to hold these rehearsals when the real pirates were out of the way: it was not so much that they feared the criticism of the professional eye as that it was not yet openly recognised what they were; and all the children shared Emily's instinct that it was better to pretend not to know—a sort of magical belief, at bottom.

Although Laura and Rachel were thrown together a great deal, and were all one goddess to Harry, their inner lives differed in almost every respect. It was a matter of principle, as will have been noticed, for them to disagree on every point; but it was a matter of nature too. Rachel had only two activities. One was domestic. She was never happy unless surrounded by the full paraphernalia of a household: she left houses and families wherever she went. She collected bits of oakum and the moultings of a worn-out mop, wrapped them in rags and put them to sleep in every nook and cranny. *Guai,* who woke one of her twenty or thirty babies—worse still, should he clear it away! She could even summon up maternal feelings for a marline-spike, and would sit up aloft rocking it in her arms and crooning. The sailors avoided walking underneath: for such an infant, if dropped from a height, will find its way through the thickest skull (an accident which sometimes befalls unpopular captains).

Further, there was hardly an article of ship's use, from the windlass to the bosun's chair, but she had metamorphosed it into some sort of furniture—a table or a bed or a lamp or a tea-set—and marked it as her property; and what she had marked as her property no one might touch —if she could prevent it. To parody Hobbes, she claimed as her own whatever she had mixed her imagination with; and the greater part of her time was spent in angry or tearful assertions of her property-rights.

Her other interest was moral. She had an extraordinary, vivid, simple sense, that child, of Right and Wrong—it almost amounted to a precocious ethical genius. Every action, her own or anyone else's, was immediately judged good or bad, and uncompromisingly praised or blamed. She was never in doubt.

To Emily, Conscience meant something very different. She was still only half aware of that secret criterion within her: but she was terrified of it. She had not Rachel's clear divination: she never knew when she might offend this inner harpy, Conscience, unwittingly: and lived in terror of those brazen claws, should she ever let it be hatched from the egg. When, poor child, she felt its latent strength stir in its pre-natal sleep, she forced her mind to other things, and would not even let herself recognise her fear of it. But she knew, at the bottom of her heart she *knew*, that one day some action of hers would rouse it, something awful done quite unwittingly would send it raging round her soul like a whirlwind. She might go weeks together in a happy unconsciousness, she might have flashes of vision when she knew she was God Himself: but at the same time she knew, beyond all doubt, in her innermost being, that she was damned: that there never had been anyone as wicked as her since the world began.

Not so Rachel: to her, Conscience was by no means so depressing an affair. It was simply a comfortable mainspring of her life, smooth-working, as pleasant as a healthy appetite. For instance, it was now tacitly admitted that all these men were pirates. That is, they were wicked. It therefore devolved on her to convert them: and she entered on her plans for this without a shadow of either misgiving or reluctance. Her conscience gave her no pain because it never occurred to her as conceivable that she should do anything but follow its dictates, or fail to see them clearly. She would try and convert these people, first: probably they would reform, but if they did not—well, she would send for the police. Since either result was right, it mattered not at all which Circumstance should call for.

So much for Rachel. The inside of Laura was different indeed: something vast, complicated and nebulous that can hardly be put into language. To take a metaphor from tadpoles, though legs were growing her gills had not yet dropped off. Being nearly four years old she was certainly a child: and children are human (if one allows the term "human" a wide sense): but she had not altogether ceased to be a baby: and babies of course are not human—they are animals, and have a very ancient and ramified culture, as cats have, and fishes, and even snakes: the same in kind as these, but much more complicated and vivid, since babies are, after all, one of the most developed species of the lower vertebrates.

In short, babies have minds which work in terms and categories of their own which cannot be translated into the terms and categories of the human mind.

It is true they look human—but not so human, to be quite fair, as many monkeys.

Subconsciously, too, everyone recognises they are animals—why else do people always laugh when a baby does some action resembling the human, as they would at a praying mantis? If the baby was only a less-developed man, there would be nothing funny in it, surely.

Possibly a case might be made out that children are not human either: but I should not accept it. Agreed that their minds are not just more ignorant and stupider than ours, but differ in kind of thinking (are *mad*, in fact): but one can, by an effort of will and imagination, think like a child at least in a partial degree—and even if one's success is infinitesimal it invalidates the case: while one can no more think like a baby, in the smallest respect, than one can think like a bee.

How then can one begin to describe the inside of Laura, where the child-mind lived in the midst of the familiar relics of the baby-mind, like a Fascist in Rome?

When swimming under water, it is a very sobering thing suddenly to look a large octopus in the face. One never forgets it: one's respect, yet one's feeling of the hopelessness of any real intellectual sympathy. One is soon reduced to mere physical admiration, like any silly painter, of the cow-like tenderness of the eye, of the beautiful and infinitesimal mobility of that large and toothless mouth, which accepts as a matter of course that very water against which you, for your life's sake, must be holding your breath. There he reposes in a fold of rock, apparently weightless in the clear green medium but very large, his long arms, suppler than silk, coiled in repose, or stirring in recognition of your presence. Far above, everything is bounded by the surface of the air, like a bright window of glass. Contact with a small baby can conjure at least an echo of that feeling in those who are not obscured by an uprush of maternity to the brain.

Of course it is not really so cut-and-dried as all this; but often the only way of attempting to express the truth is to build it up, like a card-house, of a pack of lies.

It was only in Laura's inner mind, however, that these elaborate vestiges of babyhood remained: outwardly she appeared fully a child—a rather reserved, odd, and indeed rather captivating one. Her face was not pretty, with its heavy eyebrows and reduced chin: but she had a power of apt movement, the appropriate attitude for every occasion that was most striking. A child who can show her affection for you, for instance, in the very way she plants her feet on the ground has a liberal gift of that bodily genius called charm. Actually, this particular one was a rare gesture with her: nine-tenths of her life being spent in her own head, she seldom had time to feel at all strongly either for or against people. The feelings she thus expressed were generally of a more impersonal kind, and would have fascinated an admirer of the ballet: and it was all the more remarkable that she had developed a dog-like devotion to the reserved and coarse-looking captain of the pirates.

No one really contends that children have any insight into character: their likings are mostly imaginative, not intuitive. "What do you think I am?" the exasperated ruffian had asked on a famous occasion. One might well ask what Laura thought he was: and there is no means of knowing.

2

Pigs grow quickly, quicker even than children: and much though the latter altered in the first month on board, the little black porker (whose name by the by was Thunder) altered even more. He soon grew to such a size one could not possibly allow him to lie on one's stomach any more: so, as his friendliness did not diminish, the functions were reversed, and it became a common thing to find one child, or a whole bench of them, sitting on his scaly side. They grew very fond of him indeed (especially Emily)) and called him their Dear Love, their Only Dear, their Own True Heart, and other names. But he had only two things he ever said. When his back was being scratched he enunciated an occasional soft and happy grunt; and that same phrase (only in a different tone) had to serve for every other occasion and emotion—except one. When a particularly heavy lot of children sat down on him at once, he uttered the faintest ghost of a little moan, as affecting as the wind in a very distant chimney, as if the air in him was being squeezed out through a pin-hole.

One cannot wish for a more comfortable seat than an acquiescent pig.

"If I was the Queen," said Emily, "I should most certainly have a pig for a throne."

"Perhaps she has," suggested Harry.

"He *does* like being scratched," she added presently, in a very sentimental tone, as she rubbed his scurfy back.

The mate was watching:

"I should think *you'd* like being scratched, if your skin was in that condition!"

"Oh how dis*gust*ing you are!" cried Emily, delighted.

But the idea took root:

"I don't think I should kiss him quite so much if I was you," Emily presently advised Laura, who was lying with her arms tight round his neck and covering his briny snout with kisses from ring to ears.

"My pet! My love!" murmured Laura, by way of indirect protest.

The wily mate had foreseen that some estrangement would be necessary if they were ever to have fresh pork served without salt tears. He intended this to be the thin end of the wedge. But alas! Laura's mind was as humoursome an instrument to play as the Twenty-three-stringed Lute.

When dinnertime came, the children mustered for their soup and biscuit.

They were not overfed on the schooner: they were given little that is generally considered wholesome, or to contain vitamins (unless these lurked in the aforesaid peck of dirt): but they seemed none the worse. First the cook boiled the various non-perishable vegetables they carried together in a big pot, for a couple of hours. Then a lump of salt beef from the cask forward, having been rinsed in a little fresh water, was added, and allowed to simmer with the rest till it was just cooked. Then it was withdrawn, and the captain and mate ate their soup first and their meat afterwards, out of plates, like gentlemen. After that, if it was a weekday, the meat was put to cool on the cabin shelf, ready to warm up in tomorrow's soup, and the crew and children ate the liquor with biscuit: but if it was Sunday, the captain took the lump of meat and with a benevolent air cut it up in small pieces, as if indeed for a nursery, and mixed it up with the vegetables in the huge wooden bowl out of which crew and children all dipped. It was a very patriarchal way of feeding.

Even at dinner Margaret did not join the others, but ate in the cabin, though there were only two plates on the whole ship. Probably she used the mate's when he had finished.

Laura and Rachel fought that day to tears over a particularly succulent piece of yam. Emily let them. To make those two agree was a task she was wise not to undertake. Besides, she was very busy over her own dinner. Edward managed to silence them however by declaring, in a most terrible voice, "Shut up or I'll SABRE you!"

Emily's estrangement from the captain had reached by now a rather uncomfortable stage. When these things are fresh and new the two parties avoid meeting, and all is well: but after some days they are apt to forget, find themselves on the point of chatting and then suddenly remember that they are not on speaking-terms and have to retire in confusion. Nothing can be more uncomfortable for a child. The difficulty of effecting a reconciliation in this case was that both parties felt wholly in the wrong. Each repented the impulse of a momentary insanity, and neither had an inkling the other felt the same: thus each waited for the other to show signs of forgiveness. Moreover, while the captain had far the more serious reason for being ashamed of himself, Emily was naturally far the more sensitive and concerned of the two: so it about balanced. Thus, if Emily rushed blithely up to the captain embracing a flying-fish, caught his eye and slunk round the other side of the galley, he put it down to a permanent feeling of condemnation and repulsion, blushed a deep purple and stared stonily at his wrinkling mainsail—and Emily wondered if he was *never* going to forget that bitten thumb.

But this afternoon things came to a head. Laura was trotting about behind him, striking her attitudes. Edward had at last discovered which was windward and which was leeward, and had come hot-foot to learn the first of the Sovereign Rules of Life: and Emily, with one of her wretched lapses of memory, was all agog at his elbow.

Edward was duly catechised and passed.

"Dis is the first rule," said the captain: *"Never throw anything to windward except hot water or ashes."*

Edward's face developed exactly the look of bewilderment that was intended.

"But *windward* is . . ." he began: "I mean, wouldn't they blow. . . ." Then he stopped, wondering if he had got the terms the right way round after all. Jonsen was delighted at the success of this ancient joke. Emily, trying to stand on one leg, bewildered also, lost her balance and clutched at Jonsen's arm. He looked at her—they all looked at her.

Much the best way of escaping from an embarrassing rencontre, when to walk away would be an impossible strain on the nerves, is to retire in a series of somersaults. Emily immediately started turning head over heels up the deck.

It was very difficult to keep direction, and the giddiness was appalling: but she *must* keep it up till she was out of sight, or die.

Just then Rachel, who was up the mainmast, dropped, for the first time, her marline-spike. She uttered a terrible shriek—for what *she* saw was a baby falling to dash its brains out on the deck.

Jonsen gave an ineffectual little grunt of alarm—men never can learn to give a full-bodied scream like a woman.

But Emily gave the most desperate yell of all, though several seconds after the other two: for the wicked steel stood quivering in the deck, having gouged a track through her calf on the way. Her wrought-up nerves, and sickening giddiness, joined with the shock and pain to give a heart-rending poignancy to her crying. Jonsen was by her in a second, caught her up, and carried her sobbing miserably down into the cabin. There sat Margaret, bending over some mending, her slim shoulders hunched up, humming softly and feeling deadly ill.

"Get out!" said Jonsen, in a low, brutal voice. Without a word or sign Margaret gathered up her sewing and climbed on deck.

Jonsen smeared some Stockholm tar on a rag, and bound up Emily's leg with more than a little skill, though the tar of course was agonising to her. She had cried herself right out by the time he laid her in his bunk. When she opened her streaming eyes and saw him bending over her, nothing in his clumsy face but concern and an almost overpowering pity, she was so full of joy at being at last forgiven that she reached up her arms and kissed him. He sat down on the locker, rocking himself backwards and forwards gently. Emily dozed for a few minutes; when she woke up he was still there.

"Tell me about when you were little," she said.

Jonsen sat on, silent, trying to project his unwieldy mind back into the past.

"When I was a boy," he said at last, "it wasn't thought lucky to grease your own seaboots. My Auntie used to grease mine, before we went out with the lugger."

He paused for some time.

"We divided the fish up into six shares—one for the boat, and one for each of us."

That was all. But it was of the greatest interest to Emily, and she shortly fell asleep again, supremely happy.

So for several days the captain and mate had to share the latter's bunk, Box-and-Cox; Heaven knows what hole Margaret was banished to. The gash in Emily's leg was one which would take some time to heal. To make things worse, the weather became very unsteady: when she was awake she was all right, but if she fell asleep she began to roll about the bunk, and then of course the pain waked her again; which soon reduced her to a feverish and nervous condition, although the leg itself was going on as well as could be expected. The other children of course used to come and see her; but they did not enjoy it much, as there was nothing to do down in the cabin, once the novelty of admittance to the Holy Place had worn off. So their visits were perfunctory and short. They must have had a high old time at night, however, by themselves in the forehold, now that the cat was away. They looked like it, too, in the mornings.

Otto used sometimes to come and teach her to make fancy knots, and at the same time pour out his grievances against the captain, though these latter were always received with an uncomfortable silence. Otto was a Viennese by birth, but had stowed away in a Danube barge when he was ten years old, had taken to the sea, and thereafter generally served in English ships. The only place since his childhood where he had ever spent any considerable time on shore was Wales. For some years he had sailed coastwise from the once-promising harbour of Portdinlleyn, which is now practically dead: and so, as well as German, Spanish, and English, could talk Welsh fluently. It was not a long residence, but at an impressionable age; and when he talked to Emily of his past it was mostly of his life as a "boy" on the slate-boats. Captain Jonsen came of a Danish family settled on the Baltic coast, at Lübeck. He too had spent most of his time on English ships. How or when he and Otto had first met, or how they had drifted into the Cuban piracy business, Emily never discovered. They had plainly been inseparable for many years. She preferred letting them ramble on, to asking questions or trying to fit things together: she had that sort of mind.

When the knots palled, José sent her a beautiful crochet-hook he had carved out of a beef bone: and by pulling threads out of a piece of sail-cloth she was able to set to work crocheting doilies for the cabin table. But I am afraid that she also drew a lot, till the whole of the inside of the bunk was soon as thoroughly scribbled over as a palæolithic cave. What the captain would say when he found out was a consideration best postponed. The fun was to find knots, and unevennesses in the paint, that looked like something; and then with a pencil make them look more like it—putting an eye in the walrus, or supplying the rabbit with his missing ear. That is what artists call having a proper feeling for one's material.

Instead of getting better the weather got worse: and the universe soon became a very unstable place indeed: it became almost impossible to crochet. She had to cling on to the side of the bunk all the time, to prevent her leg getting banged.

It was in this inconvenient weather, however, that the pirates chose at last to make another capture. It turned out not a rich one: a small Dutch steamer, taking a con-signment of performing animals to one of Mr. Barnum's predecessors. The captain of the steamer, who was con-ceited in a way that only certain Dutchmen *can* be con-ceited, gave them a lot of trouble, in spite of the fact that he had practically nothing worth taking. He was a first-class sailor: but he was very fair, and had no neck. In the end they had to tie him up, bring him on board the schooner, and lay him on the cabin floor where Emily could keep an eye on him. He reeked of some particularly nauseous brand of cigars, that made her head swim.

The other children had played quite an important part in the capture. They did far better as a badge of innocu-

ousness than even the "ladies." The steamer (little more
than dressed-up sailing vessels they were then), thoroughly disgruntled at the weather, was wallowing about
like a porpoise, her decks awash and her funnel over one
ear, so to speak: so when a boat put out from the
schooner, its departure cheered lustily by Edward, Harry,
Rachel and Laura, though his pride might resent it the
Dutchman never thought of suspecting this presumable
offer of assistance, and let them come on board.

It was then he began to give trouble, and they had to
remove him onto the schooner. Their tempers were none
too good on finding their booty was a lion, a tiger, two
bears and a lot of monkeys: so it is quite likely they were
none too gentle with him in transit.

The next thing was to discover whether the *Thelma,*
like the *Clorinda,* carried another, a secret cargo of
greater value. They had imprisoned all the crew, now, aft:
so one by one they were brought up on deck and questioned. But either there was no money on board, or the
crew did not know of it, or would not tell. Most of them,
indeed, appeared frightened enough to have sold their
grandmothers: but some of them simply laughed at the
pirates' bogey-bogey business, guessing they drew the line
at murder in cold blood, sober.

What was done in each case was the same. When each
man was finished with he was sent forward and shut in
the fo'c'sle: and before bringing another up from aft one
of the pirates would unmercifully belabour a roll of sail-
cloth with a cat-o'-nine-tails while another yelled like the
damned. Then a shot was fired in the air, and something
thrown overboard to make a splash. All this, of course,
was to impress those still down in the cabin awaiting their
turns: and the pretence was quite as effective as the reality

could have been. But it did no good, since probably there
was no treasure to disclose.

There was, however, a plentiful supply of Dutch spirits
and liqueurs on board: and these they found a welcome
change after so much West Indian rum.

After they had been drinking them for an hour or two
Otto had a brilliant idea. Why not give the children a
circus? They had begged and begged to be taken onto the
steamer to see the animals. Well, why not stage something
really magnificent for them—a fight between the lion and
the tiger, for instance?

No sooner said than done. The children, and every man
who could be spared, came onto the steamer, and took up
positions at safe heights in the rigging. The cargo-gaff was
rigged, the hatch opened, and the two iron cages, with
their stale cat-like reek, were hauled up on deck. Then the
little Malay keepers, who kept twittering to each other in
their windy tones, were made to open them, that the two
monarchs of the jungle might come out and do battle.

How they were to be got in again was a question that
never occurred to anyone. Yet it is generally supposed to
be easier to let tigers out of cages than to put them back.

In this case however, even when the cages were open,
neither of the beasts seemed very anxious to get out. They
lay on the floor growling (or groaning) slightly, but making no move except to roll their eyes.

It was very unfortunate for poor Emily that she was
missing all this, laid by the leg in Jonsen's stuffy cabin
with the Dutch captain to guard.

When at first they had been left alone together he had
tried to speak to her; but unlike so many Dutchmen, he
did not know a word of English. He could just move his
head, and he kept turning his eyes first on a very sharp

knife which some idiot had dropped in a corner of the cabin floor, then on Emily. He was asking her to get it for him, of course.

But Emily was terrified of him. There is something much more frightening about a man who is tied up than a man who is not tied up—I suppose it is the fear he may get loose.

The feeling of not being able to get out of the bunk and escape added the true nightmare panic.

Remember that he had no neck, and the cigar-reek.

At last he must have caught the look of fear and disgust in her face, where he had expected compassion. He began to act for himself. First gently rocking his bound body from side to side, he set himself to roll.

Emily screamed for help, beating with her fist on the bunk: but none came. Even the sailors who were left on board were out of ear-shot: they were straining all their attention to see what was happening on the steamer, that wallowed and heaved seventy yards away. There, one of the pirates, greatly daring, had descended to the rail and begun throwing belaying-pins at the cages, to rouse their occupants. If the beasts so much as lashed their tails in response, however, he would scuttle up any rope like a frightened mouse. Only the Malay keepers remained permanently on deck, taking no notice: sitting on their heels in a ring and crooning discordantly through their noses. Probably they felt inside much as the lion and tiger did.

After some minutes, however, the pirates grew bolder. Otto came right up to one cage, and started poking the tiger's ribs with a handspike. But the poor beast was far too sea-sick to be roused even by that. Gradually the whole crowd of spectators descended onto the deck and stood round, still not unprepared to bolt, while the

drunken mate, and even Captain Jonsen (who was perfectly sober), goaded and jeered.

It was not surprising no one heard poor Emily, left
alone in the cabin with the terrible Dutchman.

She screamed and screamed: but there was no awaken-
ing from *this* nightmare.

By now he had managed to roll himself, in spite of the
motion of the vessel, almost within reach of the coveted
knife. The veins on his forehead stood out with his exer-
tion and the stricture of his bonds. His fingers were groping, behind his back, for the edge.

Emily, beside herself with terror, suddenly became possessed by the strength of despair. In spite of the agony it
caused her leg she flung herself out of the bunk, and just
managed to seize the knife before he could manoeuvre his
bound hands within reach of it.

In the course of the next five seconds she had slashed
and jabbed at him in a dozen places: then, flinging the
knife towards the door, somehow managed to struggle
back into the bunk.

The Dutchman, bleeding rapidly, blinded with his own
blood, lay still and groaned. Emily, her own wound re-
opened and overcome with pain and terror, fainted. The
knife, flung wildly, missed its aim and clattered down the
steps again onto the cabin floor: and the first witness of
the scene was Margaret, who presently peered down from
the deck above, her dulled eyes standing out from her
small, skull-like face.

As for Jonsen and Otto, unable by other means to rouse
the dormant animals, they collected their men and with
big levers managed to tilt the cages, spilling the beasts out
onto the deck.

But not even so would they fight—or even show signs of resentment. As they had lain and groaned in their cages, so they now lay and groaned on the deck.

They were small specimens of their kind, and emaciated by travel. Otto with a sudden oath seized the tiger round its middle and hauled it upright on its hind legs: Jonsen did the same by the more top-heavy lion: and so the two principals to the duel faced each other, their heads lolling over the arms of their seconds.

But in the eyes of the tiger a slight ember of consciousness seemed to smoulder. Suddenly it tautened its muscles: a slight effort, yet it burst from the merely human grip of Otto like Samson from the new ropes—nearly dislocating his arms before he had time to let go. Quicker than eye could see it had cuffed him, rending half his face. Tigers are no playthings. Jonsen dropped the huge bulk of the lion on top of it, and escaped with Otto through an open door: while the pirates, tumbling over one another like people in a burning theatre, struggled to get back in the rigging.

The lion rolled clear. The tiger, lurching unsteadily, crept back into its cage. The keening Malays took no notice of the whole scene.

And yet, what a scene it had been!

But now the heroic circus was over. Chastened, bruising one another in their panic, the drunken pirates helped the mate into the first of the two boats, and pulling helter-skelter in the choppy sea, returned to the schooner. One by one they climbed the rail and vaulted on deck.

Sailors have keen noses. They smelt blood at once, and crowded round the companionway, where Margaret still sat, as if numb, on the top step.

Emily lay in the bunk below, her eyes shut—conscious again, but her eyes shut.

The Dutch captain they could see on the floor, stretched in a pool of blood. *"But, Gentlemen, I have a wife and children!"* he suddenly said in Dutch, in a surprised and gentle tone: then died, not so much of any mortal wound as the number of superficial gashes he had received.

It was plainly Margaret who had done it—killed a bound, defenceless man, for no reason at all: and now sat watching him die, with her dull, meaningless stare.

CHAPTER EIGHT

The contempt they already felt for Margaret, their complete lack of pity in her obvious illness and misery, had been in direct proportion to the childhood she had belied.

This crime would have seemed to them grave on the part of a grown man, in its unrelieved wantonness: but done by one of her years, and nurture, it was unspeakable. She was lifted by the arms from the stair where she still sat, and without a moment's hesitation (other than that resulting from too many helping hands) was dropped into the sea.

But yet the expression of her face, as—like the big white pig in the squall—she vanished to windward, left a picture in Otto's mind he never forgot. She was, after all, his affair.

The Dutchman's body was fetched up on deck. Captain Jonsen went below, and once bent over poor little Emily. She screwed up her eyes tighter when she felt his hot breath on her face. She did not open them till everybody

134

had quite gone—and shut them again when presently José came to swab the cabin floor.

The second boat, bringing back the rest of the crew and the four children, almost ran into Margaret before they saw her. She was swimming desperately, but in complete silence: her hair now plastered across her eyes and mouth, now floating out on the water as her head went under. They lifted her into the boat and set her in the sternsheets with the other children. So it was they found themselves together again.

In her sopping condition, the others naturally gave her elbow-room: but still, she was *among* them. They sat and stared at her, their eyes very wide and serious, but without speaking. Margaret, her teeth chattering with exhaustion, tried ineffectually to wring out the hem of her frock. She did not speak either: but nevertheless it was not long before both she and the other children felt a sort of thaw setting in between them.

As to the oarsmen, they never troubled their heads as to how she came in the water. They supposed she had accidentally slipped over the side: but were not particularly interested, especially as they had their work cut out manoeuvring round to the schooner's lee and clambering on board. There was a tremendous pow-wow going on aft, so that no one noticed them arrive.

Once on board, Margaret went straight forward as of old, climbed down the ladder into the fore-hold, and undressed, the other children watching her every movement with an unfeigned interest. Then she rolled herself in a blanket, and lay down.

They none of them noticed quite how it happened, but in less than half an hour they were all five absorbed in a game of Consequences. Presently one of the crew came, peered down the hatch and then shouted "Yes!" to the rest, and then went away again. But they neither saw nor heard him.

From now on, however, the atmosphere of the schooner suffered a change. A murder is inclined to have this effect on a small community. As a matter of fact, the Dutch captain's was the first blood to be shed on board, in the course of business at any rate (I will not answer for private quarrels). The way it had been shed left the pirates profoundly shocked, their eyes opened to a depravity of human nature they had not dreamt of: but also it gave them an uncomfortable feeling round the neck. So long as there was only the circus-prank to avenge, no American man-of-war was likely to be despatched in their pursuit: high Naval Authorities shrink naturally from any contact with the ridiculous: but suppose the steamer put into port, and announced the forcible abduction of her captain? Or worse, suppose her mate, with an accursed spyglass, had seen that captain's bloody body take its last dive? Pursuit would be only too likely.

The plea "It was none of us men did this wicked deed but one of our young female prisoners" was hardly one which could be submitted to a jury.

Captain Jonsen had discovered from the steamer's log where he was: so he put the schooner about, and set a course for his refuge at Santa Lucia. It was unlikely, he thought, now, that any British man-of-war would still be cruising about the scene of the *Clorinda* episode—they had too much to do: and he had reasons (fairly expensive ones) for not anticipating any molestation from the Spanish authorities. He did not like going home with an empty ship, of course: but that appeared inevitable.

The outward sign of this change in the atmosphere of the schooner was a spontaneous increase in the strictness of discipline. Not a drop of rum was drunk. Watch was kept with the regularity of a line-of-battle ship. The schooner became tidier, more seamanlike in every way.

Thunder was slain and eaten, the next day, without any regard for the feelings of his lovers: indeed, all tenderness towards the children vanished. Even José ceased playing with them. They were treated with a detached severity not wholly divorced from fear—as if these unfortunate men at last realised what diabolic yeast had been introduced into their lump.

So sensible were the children themselves of the change that they even forgot to mourn for Thunder—excepting Laura, whose face burned an angry red for half a day.

But the ship's monkey, on the other hand, with no pig now to tease, nearly died of ennui.

2

The reopening of the wound in her leg made it several days more before Emily was fit to be moved from the cabin. During this time she was much alone. Jonsen and Otto seldom came below, and when they did were too preoccupied to heed her blandishing. She sang, and conversed to herself, almost incessantly; only interrupting herself to beseech these two, with a superfluity of endearments, to pick up her crochet hook, to look at the animal she had built out of her blanket, to tell her a story, to tell her what naughty things they did when they were little —how unlike Emily it was, all this gross bidding for attention! But as a rule they went away again, or went to sleep, without taking the least notice of her.

As well, she told herself, to herself, endless stories: as
many as there are in the Arabian Nights, and quite as
involved. But the strings of words she used to utter aloud
had nothing to do with this; I mean that when she made
a sort of narrative noise (which was often), she did it for
the noise's sake: the silent, private formation of sentences
and scenes, in one's head, is far preferable for real story-
telling. If you had been watching her then, unseen, you
could only have told she was doing it by the dramatic
expressions of her face, and her restless flexing and tossing
—and if she had had the slightest inkling you were there,
the audible rigmarole would have started again. (No one
who has private thoughts going on in his own head is
quite sure of their not being overheard unless he is provid-
ing something else to occupy foreign ears.)

When she sang, however, it was always wordless: an
endless succession of notes, like a bird's, fixed to the first
vocable handy, and practically without tune. Not being
musical, there was never any reason for her to stop: so one
song would often go on for half an hour.

Although José had scrubbed the cabin floor as well as
he could, a large stain still remained.

At times she let her mind wander about, quite peace-
fully, in her memories of Jamaica: a period which now
seemed to her very remote, a golden age. How young she
must have been! When her imagination grew tired, too,
she could recall the Anansi stories old Sam had told her;
and they often proved the point of departure for new ones
of her own.

Also she could remember the creepy things he had told
her about duppies. How they used to tease the Negroes
about the supposed duppy at the bathing hole, the duppy
of the drowned man! It gave one an enormous sense of
power, that—not to believe in duppies.

But she found herself taking much less pleasure in duppies now than she used to.

She even once caught herself wondering what the
Dutchman's duppy would look like, all bloody, with its
head turned backwards on its shoulders and clanking a
chain . . . it was a momentary flash, the way the banished
image of Tabby had come back to her. For a moment her
head reeled: in another she was far from Jamaica, far
from the schooner, far from duppies, on a golden throne
in the remotest East.

The other children were no longer allowed in the cabin
to visit her: but when she heard their feet scampering
overhead, she often conversed with them in loud yells.
One of these yells from above told her:

"Marghie's back, you know."

"O-oh."

After that Emily was silent for a bit, her beautiful, innocent grey eyes fixed on the ear of a dwarf at the end of
her bunk. Only the slight pucker at the top of her nose
showed with what intensity she was thinking: and the
minute drops of sweat on her temples.

But it was not only when there was some outward occasion, like this, that she suffered acute distress.

Froth as she might, those times of consciousness, which
had begun with a moment of such sublime vision, were
both growing on her and losing their lustre. They were
become sinister. Life threatened to be no longer an inces-
sant, automatic discharge of energy: more and more
often, and when least expected, all that would suddenly
drop from her, and she would remember that she was
Emily, who had killed . . . and who was *here* . . . and that
Heaven alone knew what was going to happen to the incompetent little thing, by what miracle she was going to
keep her end up. . . . Whenever this happened, her stom-

ach seemed to drop away within her a hundred and fifty
feet.

She, like Laura, had one foot each side of a threshold
now. As a piece of Nature, she was practically invulnera-
ble. But as *Emily*, she was absolutely naked, tender. It
was particularly cruel that this transition should come
when so fierce a blast was blowing.

For mark this: anyone in bed, with a blanket up to her
chin, is in a measure safe. She might go through abysms of
terror; but once these passed, no practical harm had been
done. But once she was up and about? Suppose it was at
some crisis, some call to action that her Time came on
her? What appalling blunder could she fail to make?

Oh why must she grow up? Why, for pity's sake?

Quite apart from these attacks of blind, secret panic,
she had other times of an ordinary, very rational anxiety.
She was ten and a half now. What sort of future lay before
her, what career? (Their mother had implanted in them
young, as a matter of principle, girls and boys alike, the
idea that they would one day have to earn their own liv-
ings.) I say she was ten and a half: but it seemed such
ages since she had come on the schooner that she thought
she was probably older even than that.—Now this life was
full of interest: but was it, she asked herself, a really use-
ful education? What did it fit her for? Plainly, it taught
her nothing but to be a sort of pirate too (what sort of a
pirate, being a girl, was a problem in itself). But as time
slipped by, it became clearer and clearer that every other
life would be impossible for her—indeed, for all of them.

Gone, alas, was any shred of confidence that she was
God. That particular, supreme career was closed to her.
But the conviction that she was the wickedest person who
had ever been born, this would not die for much longer.

Some appalling Power had determined it: it was no good
struggling against it. Had she not already committed the
most awful of crimes . . . the most awful of crimes,
though, that was not murder, that was the mysterious
crime against the Holy Ghost, which dwarfed even murder . . . had she, unwittingly, at some time done this too?
She so easily might have, since she did not know what it
was. And if that were so, no wonder the pity of Heaven
was sealed against her!

So the poor little outcast lay, shivering and sweating
under her blanket, her gentle eyes fixed on the ear of the
dwarf she had drawn.

But presently she was singing again happily, and hanging right out of the bunk to outline in pencil the brown
stain on the floor. A touch here, a touch there, and it was
an old market-woman to the life, hobbling along with a
bundle on her back! I admit that it staggered even Otto, a
bit, when he came in later and saw what she had done.

But when again she lay still on her back, and contem-
plated the practical difficulties of the life ahead of her
(even leaving God and her Soul and all that on one side),
she had not the support of Edward's happy optimism: she
was old enough to know how helpless she really was. How
should she, dependent now for her very life on the kindness of those around her, how could she ever acquire the
wit and strength to struggle against them and their kind?

She had developed by this time a rather curious feeling
about Jonsen and Otto. In the first place, she had become
very fond of them. Children it is true have a way of becoming more or less attached to anyone they are in close
contact with: but it was more than that, deeper. She was
far fonder of them than she had ever been of her parents,
for instance. They, for their part, showed every mild sign

consonant with their natures of being fond of her: but
how could she *know?* It would be so easy for adult things
like them to dissemble to her, she felt. Suppose they really
intended to kill her: they could so easily hide it: they
would behave with exactly this same kindness. . . . I suppose it was the reflection of her own instinct for secretive-
ness?

When she heard the captain's step on the stairs, it
might be that he was bringing her a plate of soup, or it
might be that he had come to kill her—suddenly, with no
warning change of expression on his amiable face even at
the very end.

If that was his intention, there was nothing whatever
she could do to hinder him. To scream, struggle, attempt
flight—they would be absolutely useless, and, well, a
breach of decorum. If he chose to keep up appearances, it
behoved her to do so too. If he showed no sign of his
intention, she must show no sign of her inkling of it.

That was why, when either of them came below, she
would sing on, smile at him impishly and confidently,
actually plague him for notice.

She was a little fonder of Jonsen than of Otto. Ordi-
narily, any coarseness or malformity of adult flesh is in the
highest degree repulsive to a child: but the cracks and
scars on Jonsen's enormous hands were as interesting to
her as the valleys on the moon to a boy with a telescope.
As he clumsily handled his parallel rulers and dividers,
fitting them with infinite care to the marks on his chart,
Emily would lie on her side and explore them, give them
all names.

Why must she grow up? *Why* couldn't she leave her life
always in other people's keeping, to order as if it was no
concern of hers?

Most children have something of this feeling. With most children it is outweighed: still, they will generally hesitate before telling you they prefer to grow up. But then, most children live secure lives, and have an at least apparently secure future to grow up to. To have already murdered a full-size man, and to have to keep it for ever secret, is not a normal background for the child of ten: to have a Margaret one could not altogether banish from one's thoughts: to see every ordinary avenue of life locked against one, only a violent road, leading to Hell, open.

She was still on the border-line: so often Child still, and nothing but Child. It needed little conjuring . . . Anansi and the Blackbird, Genies and golden thrones. . . .

Which is all a rather groping attempt to explain a curious fact: that Emily appeared—indeed *was*—rather young for her age: and that this was due to, not in spite of, the adventures she had been through.

But this youngness, it burnt with an intenser flame. She had never yelled so loud at Ferndale, for sheer pleasure in her own voice, as now she yelled in the schooner's cabin, carolling like a larger, fiercer lark.

Neither Jonsen nor Otto was a nervous man; but the din she made sometimes drove them almost distracted. It was very little use telling her to shut up: she only remembered for such a short time. In a minute she was whispering, in two she was talking, in five her voice was in full blast.

Jonsen was himself a man who seldom spoke to anyone. His companionship with Otto, though devoted, was a singularly silent one. But when he did speak, he hated not to be able to make himself heard at all; even when, as was usual, it was himself he was talking to.

3

Otto was at the wheel (there was hardly one of the crew
fit to steer). His lively mind was occupied with Santa
Lucia, and his young lady there. Jonsen slipper-sloppered
up and down his side of the deck.

Presently, his interest in his subject waning, Otto's eye
was caught by the ship's monkey, which was sporting on
its back on the cabin skylight.

That animal, with the same ingenious adaptability to
circumstance which has produced the human race, had
now solved the playmate question. As a gambler will play
left hand against right, so he fought back legs against
front. His extraordinary lissomeness made the dissociation
most lifelike: he might not have been joined at the waist
at all, for all the junction discommoded him. The battle, if
good-tempered on both sides, was quite a serious one:
now, while his hind feet were doing their best to pick out
his eyes, his sharp little teeth closed viciously on his own
private parts.

From below the skylight, too, came tears and cries for
help that one might easily have taken for real, if they had
not been occasionally interrupted by such phrases as "It's
no good! I shall cut off your head just the same!"

Captain Jonsen was thinking about a little house in far-
off, shadowy Lübeck—with a china stove. It didn't do to
talk about retiring: above all, one must never say aloud
"This is my last voyage," even addressing oneself. The sea
has an ironic way of interpreting it in her own fashion, if
you do. Jonsen had seen too many skippers sail on their
"last voyage"—and never return.

He felt acutely melancholy, not very far from tears; and
presently he went below. He wanted to be alone.

Emily by now was conducting, in her head, a secret conversation with John. She had never done so before: but today he had suddenly presented himself to her imagination. Of course his disappearance was strictly taboo between them: what they chiefly discussed was the building of a magnificent raft, to use in the bathing-hole at Ferndale; just as if they had never left the place.

When she heard the captain's step, so nearly surprising her at it, she blushed a deep red. She felt her cheeks still hot when he arrived. As usual, he did not even glance at her. He plumped down on a seat, put his elbows on the cabin table, his head in his hands, and rocked it rhythmically from side to side.

"Look, Captain!" she insisted. "Do I look pretty like this? Look! *Look!* Look, *do* I look pretty like this?"

For once he raised his head, turned, and considered her at length. She had rolled up her eyes till only the whites showed, and turned her under-lip inside out. With her first finger she was squashing her nose almost level with her cheeks.

"No," he said simply, "you do not." Then he returned to his cogitation.

She stuck out her tongue as well, and waggled it.

"Look!" she went on. "Look!"

But instead of looking at her, he let his eye wander round the cabin. It seemed changed somehow—emasculated: a little girl's bedroom, not a man's cabin. The actual physical changes were tiny: but to a meticulous man, they glared. The whole place smelt of children.

Unable to contain himself, he crammed on his cap and burst up the stairs.

On deck, the others were romping round the binnacle, wildly excited.

"Damn!" cried Jonsen at the sight of them, stamping in an ungovernable rage.

Of course his slippers came off, and one of them skiddered up the deck.

What devil entered into Edward I do not know; but the sight was too much for him. He seized the slipper and rushed off with it, shrieking with delight. Jonsen roared at him: he passed it to Laura, and was soon dancing up and down at the end of the jib-boom. Edward, of all people! The timid, respectful Edward!

Laura could hardly carry the enormous thing: but she clasped it tight in her arms, lowered her head, and with the purposeful air of a rugger-player ran back with it very fast up the deck, apparently straight into Jonsen's arms. At the last moment she dodged him neatly: continued right on past Otto at the wheel, just as serious and just as fast, and forward again on the port side. Jonsen, no quick mover at any time, stood in his socks and roared himself hoarse. Otto was shaking with laughter like a jelly.

This mad intoxication, which had flashed from child to child, now dropped a spark into the crew. They were already peering excitedly from the fo'c'sle hatch, grins struggling with outrage for pride of place: but at this point they broke into a cheer. Then, like the devils in a pantomime, they all sank together through the floor, aghast at themselves, and pulled the scuttle over their heads.

Laura, still hugging the slipper, caught her toe in an eye-bolt and fell full length, setting up a yell.

Otto, with a suddenly straight face, ran forward, picked up the slipper and returned it to Jonsen, who put it on. Edward stopped jumping up and down and became frightened.

Jonsen was trembling with rage. He advanced on Edward with an iron belaying pin in his hand.

"Come down from there!" he commanded.

"Don't! Don't! Don't!" cried Edward, not moving. Harry suddenly ran and hid himself in the galley, though he had had no part in it.

With a surprising agility which he rarely used, Jonsen started out along the bowsprit towards Edward, who did nothing but moan "Don't!" at the sight of that murderous belaying pin. When Jonsen was just on him, however, he swarmed up a stay, helping himself with the iron hanks of the jib.

Jonsen returned to the deck, wringing his hands and angrier than ever. He sent a sailor to the crosstrees to head the boy off and drive him down again.

Indeed, but for an extraordinary diversion, I shudder to think what might have happened to him. But just at this moment there appeared, up the ladder from the children's forehold, Rachel. She wore one of the sailors' shirts, back to front, and reaching to her heels: in her hand, a book. She was singing "Onward, Christian Soldiers" at the top of her voice. But as soon as she reached the deck she became silent: strutted straight aft, looking neither to right nor left, genuflected to Otto at the wheel and then sat herself down on a wooden bucket.

Everyone, Jonsen included, stood petrified. After a moment of silent prayer she arose, and commenced an inarticulate gabble-gabble which reproduced extraordinarily well the sound of what she used to hear in the little church at St. Anne's, where the whole family went one Sunday in each month.

Rachel's religious revival had begun. It could hardly have been more opportune: who shall say it was not

Heaven which had chosen the moment for her?

Otto, entering into the thing at once, rolled up his eyes and spread out his arms, crosswise, against the wheel-house at his back.

Jonsen, rapidly recovering some of his temper, strode up to her. Her imitation was admirable. For a few moments he listened in silence. He wavered: should he laugh? Then what remained of his temper prevailed.

"Rachel!" he rebuked.

She continued, almost without taking breath, "Gabble-gabble, brethren, gabble-gabble."

"I am not a religious man myself," said the captain, "but I will not allow religion to be made a mock of on my ship!"

He caught hold of Rachel.

"Gabble-gabble!" she went on, slightly faster and on a higher note. "Let me alone! Gabble-gabble! Amen! Gabble . . ."

But he sat himself on the bucket, and stretched her over his knee.

"You're a wicked pirate! You'll go to Hell!" she shrieked, breaking at last into the articulate.

Then he began to smack her so hard that she screamed almost as much with pain as with rage.

When at last he set her down her face was swollen and purple. She directed a tornado of punches with her little fists against his knees, crying "Hell! Hell! Hell!" in a strangulated voice.

He flipped her fists aside with his hand, and presently she went away, so tired with crying she could hardly get her breath.

Meanwhile, Laura's behaviour had been characteristic. When she tripped and fell, she roared till her bumps ceased hurting. Then, with no perceptible transition, her convulsions of agony became an attempt to stand on her head. This she kept up throughout Edward's flight up the stay, throughout the electric appearance of Rachel. During the latter's punishment, having happened to topple in the direction of the mainmast, and finding her feet against the rack round its base for belaying the halyards to, she gave a shove off—she would roll instead. And roll she did, very rapidly, till she arrived at the captain's feet. There she lay, all the while he was smacking Rachel, completely unconcerned, on her back, her knees drawn up to her chin, humming a little tune.

4

When Emily returned to the forehold, her first act was one which greatly complicated life. As if there was not sea enough already, outside the ship, she decreed that practically all the deck was sea also. The main hatch was an island, of course; and there were others—chiefly natural excrescences of the same kind. But all the rest, all the open deck, could only be safely crossed in a boat, or swimming.

As to who was in a boat, and who wasn't, Emily decided that herself. No one ever knew till they had asked her. But Laura, once she had got the main idea into her head, always swam, whether said to be in a boat or not—to be on the safe side.

"*Isn't* she silly?" said Edward once, when she refused to stop working her arms although they had all told her she was safe on board.

"I expect we were all as silly as that, when we were young," said Harry.

It was a source of consternation to the children that none of the grown-ups would recognise this "sea". The sailors trod carelessly on the deepest oceans, refusing so much as to paddle with their hands. But it was equally irritating to the sailors when the children, either safe on an island or bearing down in a vessel of their own, would scream at them in a tone of complete conviction:

"You're drowning! You're drowning! O-o-oh, look out! You're out of your depth there! The sharks'll eat you!"

"O-oh look! Miguel's sinking! The waves are right over his head!"

That happens to be the one sort of joke sailors can't enjoy. Even though the words were unintelligible, their gist—eked out by the slightly malicious hints of the mate —was not. If they steadily refused to swim, they at least took to crossing themselves fervently and continuously whenever they had to traverse a piece of open deck. For there was no way one could be certain that these brats were not gifted with second sight—*hijos de puntas!*

What the children were really doing, of course, was trying out what it would feel like when they themselves were all grown pirates, running a joint venture or each with a craft of his own: and though they never so much as mentioned piracy in the course of these public navigations, they talked their heads off about it at night, now.

Margaret also refused to swim: but they knew by now it was no good trying to make her: no good yelling at *her* she was drowning, for all she did at that word was to sit down and cry. So it became a recognised convention that Margaret, wherever she went or whatever she was doing, was on a raft, with a keg of biscuit and a barrel of water, by herself—and could be ignored.

For, since her return, she had become very dull company. That one game of Consequences had been a flash in the pan. For several days after it she had remained in bed, hardly speaking, and inclined to tear strips off her blanket when she was asleep: and even when she was about again, though perfectly amiable—more amiable than before— she refused to join in any game whatever. She seemed happy: but for any imaginative purpose she was useless.

Moreover, she made no attempt to regain the sovereignty to which Emily had succeeded. She never ordered anyone about. There was not even any fun to be got out of baiting her: nothing seemed to ruffle her temper. She was treated sometimes with a good-humored contempt, sometimes ignored altogether: and it was enough for *her* to say something for it to be automatically voted silly.

Rachel also, for several days after her service, showed no disposition to join with the others either. She preferred to sit about below, sulking, in the hold. From time to time she attempted to pick a hole, with a copper nail she had got hold of, in the bottom of the ship, and so sink it. It was Laura who discovered her purpose, and came hot-foot to Emily with the news. Laura never doubted, any more than Rachel did, that the task was a possible one.

Emily came below, and found her at it. After three days, she had only managed to scratch up one single splinter—partly because she never attacked the same place twice: but both she and Laura expected to see quantities of water come welling through, and rapidly fill the ship. Indeed, though no water had yet appeared, Laura was convinced the ship was already perceptibly lowered as a result of Rachel's efforts.

Laura clasped her hands in expectation, waiting to see what Emily would do in the face of this impending disaster.

"You stupid, *that's* no good!" was all Emily's comment.

Rachel looked at her angrily:

"You leave me alone! I know what I am doing!"

Emily's eyes grew very wide, and danced with a strange light.

"If you talk to me like that, I'll have you hanged from the yard-arm!"

"What's *that?*" asked Rachel sulkily.

"You ought to know which is the yard-arm by now!"

"I don't care!" growled Rachel, and went on scratching with her nail.

Emily picked up a big piece of iron, in a corner, so heavy she could hardly carry it:

"Do you know what I am going to do?" she asked in a strange voice.

At the sound of it Rachel stopped scratching and looked up.

"No," she said, a trifle uneasily.

"I'm going to kill you! I'm turned a pirate, and I'm going to kill you with this sword!"

At the word "sword", the misshapen lump of metal seemed to Rachel to flicker to a sharp, wicked point.

She looked Emily in the eyes, doubtfully. Did she mean it, or was it a game?

As a matter of fact, she had always been a little afraid of Emily. Emily was so huge, so strong, so old (as good as grown up), so cunning! Emily was the cleverest, the most powerful person in the world! The muscles of a giant, the ancient experience of a serpent!—And now, her terrible eyes, with no hint in them of pretence.

Emily glared fixedly, and saw real panic dawn in Rachel's face. Suddenly the latter turned, and as fast as her short fat legs would carry her began to swarm up the ladder. Emily rang her iron once against it, and Rachel nearly tumbled down again in her haste.

The iron was so big and heavy it took Emily a long time to haul it up on deck. Even when that was done, it greatly impeded her running, so that she and Rachel did three laps round the deck without their distances altering much, cheered boisterously by Edward. Even in her terror Rachel did not forget to work her arms as in breast-stroke. Finally, with a cry of "Oh I can't run any more, my bad leg's hurting!" Emily flung down the iron and dropped panting beside Edward on the main hatch.

"I shall put poison in your dinner!" she shouted cheerfully to Rachel; but the latter retreated behind the windlass and began to nurse with an abandoned devotion the particular brood she had parked there, working herself almost to tears with the depth of her maternal pity for them.

Emily went on chuckling for some time at the memory of her sport.

"What's the matter with you?" asked Edward scornfully, puffing out his chest. He was feeling particularly manly at the moment. "Have you got the giggles?"

"I *like* having the giggles," said Emily disarmingly. "Let's see if we can't all get them. Come on Laura! Harry, come!"

The two smaller ones came obediently. They stared her in the face, attentively and seriously, awaiting the Coming of the God, while she herself broke into louder and louder explosions of laughter. Soon the infection took and they were laughing too, each shriller and more wildly than the other.

"I can't stop! I can't stop!" they cried at intervals.

"Come on, Edward! Look me in the face!"

"I won't!" said Edward.

So she set on him and tickled him, till he was as hysterical as the rest.

"Oh I *do* want to stop, my tummy is hurting so!" complained Harry at last.

"Go away, then," advised Emily in a lucid interval. And so the group presently broke up. But they had all to avoid each other's eye for a long while, if they were not to risk another attack.

It was Laura who was cured the quickest. She suddenly discovered what a beautiful deep cave her arm-pit made, and decided to keep fairies in it in future. For some while she could think of nothing else.

5

Captain Jonsen called suddenly to José to take the wheel, and went below for his telescope. Then, buttressing his hip against the rail, and extending the shade over the object glass, he stared fixedly at something almost in the eye of the setting sun. Emily, in a gentle mood, wandered up to him, and stood, her side just touching him. Then she began lightly rubbing her cheek on his coat, as a cat does.

Jonsen lowered the glass and tried his naked eye, as if he had more trust in it. Then he explored with the glass once more.

What was that businesslike-looking sail, tall and narrow as a pillar? He swept his eye round the rest of the horizon: it was empty—only that single threatening finger, pointing upwards.

Jonsen had chosen his course with care to avoid all the ordinary tracks of shipping at that time of year. Especially he had chosen it to avoid the routine-passages of the Jamaica Squadron from one British island to another. This

—it had no business here: no more than he had himself.

Emily put her arm round his waist and gave it a slight hug.

"What is it?" she said: "Do let me look."

Jonsen said nothing, continuing to stare with concentration.

"*Do* let me look!" said Emily: "I haven't ever looked through a telescope, ever!"

Jonsen abruptly snapped the glass to, and looked down at her. His usually expressionless features were stirred from their roots. He lifted one hand and gently began to stroke her hair.

"Do you love me?" he asked.

"Mm," assented Emily. Later she added, with a wriggle, "You're a darling."

"If it was to help me, would you do something . . . very difficult?"

"Yes, but *do* let me have a look through your telescope, because I haven't, not ever, and I do so want to!"

Jonsen gave a weary sigh, and sat down on the cabin-top. What *on Earth* were children's heads made of, inside?

"Now listen," he said: "I want to talk to you seriously."

"Yes," said Emily, trying to hide her extreme discomfort. Her eye plaintively searched the deck for something to hold it. He pressed her against his knee in an attempt to win her attention.

"If bad, cruel men came and wanted to kill me and take you away, what would you do?"

"Oh how horrid!" said Emily: "Will they?"

"Not if you help me."

It was unbearable. With a sudden leap she was astride his knees, her arms round his neck and her hands pressng the back of his head.

"I wonder if you make a good Cyclops?" she said; and

holding his head firmly laid her nose to his nose, her forehead to his forehead, both staring into each other's eyes,
an inch apart, till each saw the other's face growing narrow and two eyes converge to one large, misty eye in the
middle.

"Lovely!" said Emily; "You're just right for one! Only
now one of *your* eyes has got loose and is floating up
above the other one!"

The sun touched the sea, and for thirty seconds every
detail of the distant man-of-war was outlined in black
against the flame. But, for the life of him, Jonsen could
think of nothing but that house in quiet Lübeck, with
the green porcelain stove.

CHAPTER NINE

The darkness closed down with its sudden curtain
on that minatory finger.

Captain Jonsen remained on deck all night, whether it
was his watch or not. It was a hot night, even for those
latitudes: and no moon. The suffused brilliance of the
stars lit up everything close quite plainly, but showed
nothing in the distance. The black masts towered up,
clear against the jewelry, which seemed to swing slowly a
little to one side, a little to the other, of their tapering
points. The sails, the shadows in their curves all diffused
away, seemed flat. The halyards and topping-lifts and
braces showed here, were invisible there, with an arbitrar-
iness which took from them all meaning as mechanism.

Looking forward with the glowing binnacle-light at
one's back, the narrow milky deck sloped up to the fore-
shortened tilt of the bowsprit, which seemed to be trying
to point at a single enlarged star just above the horizon.

The schooner moved just enough for the sea to divide
with a slight rustle on her stem, breaking out into a
shower of sparks, which lit up also wherever the water

rubbed the ship's side, as if the ocean were a tissue of sensitive nerves; and still twinkled behind in the mere paleness of the wake. Only a faint tang of tar in the nostrils was there to remind one that this was no ivory and ebony fantasia but a machine. For a schooner is in fact one of the most mechanically satisfactory, austere, unornamented engines ever invented by Man.

A few yards off, a shoal of luminous fish shone at different depths.

But a few hundred yards off, one could see nothing! The sea became a steady glittering black, that did not seem to move. Near, one could see so much detail it seemed impossible to believe that there a whole ship might lie invisible: impossible to believe that by no glass, no anxious straining of the eyes, could one ever *see*.

Jonsen strode up and down the lee side of the vessel, so that what breeze there was, collecting in the hollow of the sails, overflowed down onto him in a continuous cool cascade. From time to time he climbed to the foremast head, in spite of the fact that added height could not possibly give added vision: stared into the blank till his eyes ached, and then came down and resumed his restless pacing. A ship with her lights out might creep within a mile of him, and he not know it.

Jonsen was not given to intuitions: but he had now an extraordinary feeling of certainty that somewhere close in that cover of darkness his enemy lay, preparing destruction for him. He strained his ears too: but he could hear nothing either, except the rustle of the water, the occasional knocking of a loose block.

If only there had been a moon! He remembered another occasion, fifteen years before. The slaver of which he was then second mate was bowling along, the hatches down on her stinking cargo, all canvas spread, when right across the glittering path of the moon a frigate crossed, almost within gun-shot—crossed the light, and disappeared again. Jonsen had realised at once that though the frigate, with the light behind it, was now invisible to them, they, with the moonlight shining full on them, would be perfectly visible to the frigate. The boom of a gun soon proved it. He had wanted to make a blind bolt for it: but his captain, instead, ordered every stitch of sail to be furled: and so they lay all night under their bare pools, not moving of course but (with nothing to reflect the light) grown invisible in their turn. When dawn came the frigate was so far down the wind they had easily shown her a clean pair of heels.

But tonight! There was no friendly moon track to betray the attacker: nothing but this inner conviction, which grew every moment more certain.

Shortly after midnight he had descended from one of his useless climbs to the masthead, and stood for a moment by the open forehatch. The warm breath of the children was easily discernible. Margaret was chattering in her sleep—quite loud, but you could not distinguish a single clear word.

Moved by a whim, Jonsen climbed down the ladder into the hold. Below, it was hot as an oven. A zooming winged cockroach cannoned about. The sound of the water, a dry rustle above, was here a pleasant gurgle and plop against the wooden shell; most musical of sounds to a sailor.

Laura lay on her back in the faint light of the open hatch. She had discarded her blanket; and the vest which did duty for a night-gown was rucked right up under her arms. Jonsen wondered how anything so like a frog could ever conceivably grow into the billowy body of a woman. He bent down and attempted to pull down the vest: but at the first touch Laura rolled violently over onto her stomach, then drew her knees up under her, thrusting her pointed rump up at him; and continued to sleep in that position, breathing noisily.

As his eyes got used to the gloom, vague white splodges showed him that most of the children had discarded their dark blankets. But he did not notice Emily, sitting up in the darkness and watching him.

As he turned to go, an experimental smile lit up his face: he bent, and gently flicked Laura's behind with his finger-nail. It collapsed like a burst balloon; but still she went on sleeping, flat on her face now.

Jonsen was still chuckling to himself as he reached the deck. But there his forebodings returned to him with re-doubled force. He could *feel* that man-of-war lying-to in the darkness, biding its time! For the fiftieth time he climbed the ratlines and took his stand at the crosstrees, skinning his eyes.

Presently, looking down, he could just discern the small white figure on the deck which was Emily, hopping and skipping about. But it passed at once out of his mind.

Suddenly his tired eye caught a patch of something darker than the sea. He looked away, then back again, to make sure. It was still there: on the port bow: impossible to make out clearly, though . . . Jonsen slid down the shrouds in a flash, like a prentice. Landing on the deck like a thunderbolt he nearly startled Emily out of her life: she had no idea he was up there. She startled him no less.

"It's so *hot* down there," she began, "I can't sleep——"

"Get below!" hissed Jonsen furiously: "Don't you dare come up again! And don't let any of the others, till I tell you!"

Emily, thoroughly frightened, tumbled down the ladder as fast as she could and rolled herself in her blanket from head to foot: partly because her bare legs were really a little chilled, but more for comfort. What had she done? What was happening? She was hardly down when feet were heard scurrying across the deck, and the hatches over her head were loosely fitted into place. The darkness was profound, and seemed to be rolling on her. No one was within reach: and she dared not move an inch. Everyone was asleep.

Jonsen called all hands on deck: and in silence they mustered at the rail. The patch was clearly visible now: nearer, and smaller than he had thought at first. They listened for the splash of oars: but it came on in silence.

Suddenly they were upon it, it was grating against the ship's side, slipping astern. It was a dead tree, carried out to sea by some river in spate, and tangled up with weed.

But after that, he kept all hands on deck till dawn. In their new mood, they obeyed him readily enough. For they knew he was not incompetent. He generally did the right thing—it was only the fuss he made in any emergency which gave him the appearance of blundering.

Yet, though there were now so many eyes watching, no further alarm was given.

But the moment the first paleness of dawn glimmered, everyone's nerves tightened to cracking-point. The rapidly increasing light would any moment show them their fate.

It was not till full daylight, however, that Jonsen would let himself be convinced there was absolutely no man-of-war there.

As a matter of fact, its royals had sunk below the horizon less than an hour after he had first sighted it.

2

But the alarm of that night caused Jonsen at last to make up his mind.

He altered his course: and as before he had designed it to avoid other shipping, now on the contrary it was calculated to run as soon as possible into the very track of the Eastward Bounders.

Otto rubbed his eyes. What had come over the fellow? Did he want revenge for the fright he had had? Was he going to try and cut out a prize right in the thick of the traffic? It would be like Jonsen, that; to put his head in the lion's mouth after trembling at its roar: and Otto's heart warmed towards him. But he asked no questions.

Meanwhile Jonsen went to his cabin, opened a secret receptacle in his bunk, and took out a job-lot of ships' papers which he had bought from a Havana dealer in such things. The *"John Dodson", of Liverpool, bound for the Seychelles with a cargo of cast-iron pots*—what use was that in these waters? The man had sold him a pup! —Ah, this was better: *"Lizzie Green", of Bristol, bound from Matanzas to Philadelphia in ballast* . . . a funny trip to make in ballast, true: but that was no one's affair but his imaginary owner's. Jonsen made sure all was in order —filled in the blank dates, and so on—then returned the bundle to its hiding place for another occasion. Coming on deck he gave a number of orders.

First, stages were rigged over the bows and stern, and José and a paint-pot went over the rail to add *Lizzie Green* to the many names which from time to time had decorated the schooner's escutcheon. Not content with that, he had it painted on every other appropriate place— the boats, the buckets—it was as well to be thorough.

Meanwhile, many of the sails were taken down and new ones bent—or rather old ones, distinctive sails that a man would swear he couldn't have forgotten if he had ever seen them before. Otto sewed a large patch to the mainsail, where there was no hole. In his zeal Jonsen even considered lowering the yards and rigging her as a pure fore-and-after: but luckily for his sweating crew abandoned the idea.

The master-stroke of his disguise was permanent—that he carried no guns. Guns can be hidden or thrown overboard, it is true: but the grooves they make in the deck cannot, as many a protesting-innocent sea-robber has found to his cost. Jonsen not only had no guns to hide, he had no grooves: any fool could see he had no guns, and never had had any. And who ever heard of a pirate without guns? It was laughable: yet he had proved, again and again, that one could make a capture just as easily without them: and further, that the captured merchantman, in making his report, could generally be counted on to imagine a greater or less display of artillery. Whether it was to save their faces, or pure conservatism—presumption that there must have been guns—nearly every vessel Jonsen had had dealings with had reported masked artillery, manned by "fifty or seventy ruffians of the worst Spanish type."

Of course if he met and was challenged by a man-of-war, he would have to give in without a fight. But then, it never pays to fight a man-of-war anyhow. If he is a big one, he sinks you. If he is some little cock-shell of a cutter, commanded by a fire-eating young officer just into his teens, you sink him—and then there is the devil to pay. Better be sunk outright than insult the honour of a great nation in that fashion.

When he at last remembered to take the hatches off the children, they were half dead with suffocation, It was hot enough, stuffy enough anyhow down there, only the square opening above for ventilation; but with the hatches even loosely in place it was a Black Hole. Emily had at last dropped asleep, and slept late, through a chain of nightmares; when she did wake in the closed hold, she sat up, then fainted immediately, and fell back, her breath coming in loud snores. Before she came to again she was already sobbing miserably. At that the little ones began to cry too: which sound it was that reminded Jonsen, rather late, to take the hatches off.

He was quite alarmed when he saw them. It was not till they had been out in the morning freshness of the deck for some time that they even summoned up interest in the strange metamorphosis of the schooner that was in progress.

Jonsen looked at them with a troubled eye. They had not indeed the appearance of well-cared-for children, though he had not noticed this before. They were dirty to a fault: their clothes torn, and mended, if at all, with twine. Their hair was not only uncombed—there was tar in it. They were mostly thin, and a yellowy-brown colour. Only Rachel remained obstinately plump and pink. The scar on Emily's leg was still a blushing purple: and they all were blotched with insect-bites.

Jonsen called José off his painting job: gave him a bucket of fresh water: the mate's (the only) comb: and a pair of scissors. José wondered innocently: they did not look to him particularly dirty. But he did his duty, while they were still too sorry for themselves to object actively, to do anything more than sob weakly when he hurt them. Even when he had finished their toilet, of course, he had not reached the point at which a nurse-maid usually begins.

It was noon before the *Lizzie Green* looked herself— whoever that might be: and a little after noon she was still heading for "Philadelphia" when, hull down on the horizon, two sail were sighted, many miles apart, at about the same minute. Captain Jonsen considered carefully; made his choice, and altered his course so as to fall in with her as soon as might be.

Meanwhile, the crew had no more doubt than Otto had of Jonsen's intention: and the sound of the whetstone floated merrily aft, till each man's knife had an edge that did its master's heart good. I have said that the murder of the Dutch captain had affected the whole character of their piracy. The yeast was working.

Presently the smoke of a large steamer cropped up over the horizon as well. Otto sniffed the breeze. It might hold, or it might not. They were still far from home, and these seas crowded. The whole enterprise looked to him pretty desperate.

Jonsen was at his usual shuffle-shuffle, nervously biting his nails. Suddenly he turned on Otto and called him below. He was plainly very agitated; his cheeks red, his eye wild. He began by plotting himself meticulously on the chart. Then he growled over his shoulder:

"Those children, they must go."

"Aye," said Otto. Then, as Jonsen said no more, he added: "You'll land them at Santa, I take it?"

"No! They must go now. We may never get to Santa."

Otto took a deep breath.

Jonsen turned on him, blustering:

"If we get taken with them, where'll *we* be, eh?"

Otto went white, then red, before he answered.

"You'll have to risk that," he said slowly. "You can't land them no other place."

"Who said I was going to land them?"

"There's nothing else you can do," said Otto stubbornly.

A light of comprehension dawned suddenly in Jonsen's worried face.

"We could sew them up in little bags," he said with a genial smile, "and put them over the side."

Otto gave him one quick glance; what he saw was enough to relieve him.

"What are you going to do?" he asked.

"Sew them up in little bags! Sew them up in little bags!" Jonsen affirmed, rubbing his hands together and chuckling, all the latent sentimentality of the man getting the better of him. Then he pushed past Otto and went on deck.

The big brigantine, which he had aimed for at first, was proving a bit too far up the wind for him: so now he took the helm and let the schooner's head down a couple of points, to intercept the steamer instead.

Otto whistled. At last an inkling of what the captain was at had dawned on him.

3

As they drew nearer, the children were all immensely interested: they had never before seen anything like this big, miraculous tub. The Dutch steamer, an old-fashioned craft, had not differed very materially from a sailing-vessel: but this, in form, was already more like the steamers of our own day. Its funnel was still tall and narrow, with a kind of artichoke on top, it is true: but otherwise it was much the same as you and I are used to.

Jonsen spoke her urgently: and presently her engines stopped. The *Lizzie Green* slipped round under her lee. Jonsen had a boat lowered: then embarked in it himself. The children and the schooner's crew stood at the rail in tense excitement: watched a little ladder lowered from her towering iron side: watched Jonsen, alone, in his dark Sunday suit and the peaked cap of his rank, climb on board. He had timed it nicely: in another hour it would be dark.

He had no easy task. First he had his premeditated fiction to establish, his explanation of how he came by his passengers. Secondly, he had to persuade the captain of the steamship, a stranger, to relieve him, where he had so signally failed to persuade his friend the señor at Santa Lucia.

Otto was not a man to show agitation: but he felt it, nonetheless. This scheme of Jon's was the foolhardiest thing he had ever heard of: the slightest suspicion, and they were as good as done for.

Jonsen had ordered him, if he guessed anything was wrong, to run.

Meanwhile, the breeze was dropping, and it was still daylight.

Jonsen had vanished into the steamer as into a forest.

Emily was as excited as any of them, pointing out the novel features of this extraordinary vessel. The children still thought it was professional quarry. Edward was openly bragging of what he would do when he had captured it.

"I shall cut the captain's head off and throw it in the water!" he declared aloud.

"S-s-sh!" exclaimed Harry, in a stage whisper.

"Coo! I don't care!" cried Edward, intoxicated with

bravado: "Then I shall take out all the gold and keep it for myself."

"I shall sink it!" said Harry, in imitation: then added as an afterthought, "Right to the very bottom!"

Emily fell silent, her peculiarly vivid imagination having the mastery of her. She saw the hold of the steamer, piled with gold and jewels. She saw herself, fighting her way through hordes of hairy sailors, with her bare fists, till only the steamer's captain stood between her and the treasure.

Then it happened! It was as if a small cold voice inside her said suddenly: *"How can you? You're only a little girl!"* She felt herself falling giddily from the heights, shrinking. She was *Emily*.

The awful, blood-covered face of the Dutch captain seemed to threaten her out of the air. She cowered back at the shock. But it was over in a moment.

She looked around her in terror. Did anyone know how defenceless she was? Surely someone must have noticed her. The other children were gibbering in their animal innocence. The sailors, their knives half concealed, grinned at each other or cursed. Otto, his brows knotted, stood with his eyes fixed on the steamer.

She feared everybody, she hated everybody.

Margaret was whispering something to Edward, and he nodded. Again panic seized her. What was Margaret telling him? Had she told everyone? Did they all know? Were they all playing with her, deceiving her by pretending not to know, waiting their own time to burst their revelation on her and punish her in some quite unimaginably awful way?

Had Margaret told? If she crept up behind Margaret now, and pushed her in the sea, might she yet be in time?

—But even as she thought it, she seemed to see Margaret rising waist-high out of the waves, telling the whole story to everybody in a calm, dispassionate voice, and climbing back on board.

In another flash she saw the fat, comfortable person of her mother, standing at the door of Ferndale, abusing the cook.

Again her eyes roamed round the sinister reality of the schooner. She suddenly felt sick to death of it all: tired, beyond words tired. Why must she be chained for ever to this awful life? Could she never escape, never get back to the ordinary life little girls lead, with their papas and mamas and . . . birthday cakes?

Otto called her. She went to him obediently; though with a presentiment that it was to her execution. He turned, and called Margaret too.

She was in a more attentive mood than she had been the night before with the captain, Heaven knows! But Otto was too pre-occupied to notice how frightened her eyes were.

Jonsen had no easy task on the steamer: but Otto did not greatly relish his own. He did not know how to begin —and everything depended on his success.

"See here," he burst out: "You're going to England."

Emily shot him a quick glance. "Yes?" she said at last: her voice showing merely a polite interest.

"The captain has gone onto that steamboat, to arrange about it."

"Aren't we staying with you any longer, then?"

"No," said Otto: "you're going home on that steamboat."

"Shan't we see you any more, then?" Emily pursued.

"No," said Otto: "—Well, someday, perhaps."

"Are they all going, or only us two?"

"Why, all of you of course!"

"Oh. I didn't know."

There was an awkward silence, while Otto wondered how to tackle the real problem.

"Had we better go and get ready?" asked Margaret.

"Now listen!" Otto interrupted her. "When you get on board, they'll ask you all about everything. They'll want to know how you got here."

"Are we to tell them?"

Otto was astonished she took his point so readily.

"No," he said. "The captain and me don't want you to. We want you to keep it a secret, do you see?"

"What *are* we to say, then?" Emily asked.

"Tell them . . . you were captured by pirates, and then . . . they put you ashore at a little port in Cuba——"

"—Where the Fat Woman was?"

"—Yes. And then we came along, and took you on board our schooner, which was going to America, to save you from the pirates."

"I see," said Emily.

"You'll say that, and keep the . . . other a secret?" Otto asked anxiously.

Emily gave him her peculiar, gentle stare.

"Of course!" she said.

Well, he had done his best: but Otto felt heavy at heart. That little cherub! He didn't believe she could keep a secret for ten seconds.

"Now: do you think you can make the little ones understand?"

"Oh yes, I'll tell them," said Emily easily. She considered for a moment: "I don't suppose they remember much anyway.—Is that all?"

"That's all," said Otto; and they walked away.

"What was he saying?" Margaret asked. "What was it all about?"

"Oh shut up!" said Emily rudely: "It's nothing to do with you!"

But inwardly, she did not know whether she was on her head or her heels. Were they really going to let her escape? Weren't they just tantalising her, meaning to stop her at the last moment? Were they handing her over to strangers, who had come to hang her for murder? Was her mother perhaps on that steamer, come to save her? But she loved Jonsen and Otto: how could she bear to part with them? The dear, familiar schooner. . . . All these thoughts in her head at once! But she dealt firmly enough with the Liddlies:

"Come on!" she said: "We're going on that steamer."

"Are *we* to do the fighting?" Edward asked, timorously enough.

"There isn't going to be any fighting," said Emily.

"Will there be another circus?" asked Laura.

Then she told them they were to change ships again.

When Captain Jonsen came back, mopping the sweat from his polished forehead with a big cotton handkerchief, he seemed in a terrible hurry. As for the children, they were so excited they were ready to tumble into the boat: in such a flurry they nearly tumbled into the sea instead. *Now* they knew why they had been washed and combed.

It did not seem at first as if there was going to be any difficulty about getting them started. But it was Rachel who began the break-away:

"My babies! My babies!" she shrieked, and began running all over the ship, routing out bits of rag, fuzzy rope-ends, paint-pots . . . her arms were soon full.

"Here, you can't take all that junk!" dissuaded Otto.

"Oh but my darlings, I can't leave you behind!" cried
Rachel piteously. Out rushed the cook, just in time to
retrieve his ladle—and a battle-royal began.

Naturally, Jonsen was on tenterhooks to be gone. But it
was essential they should part on good terms.

José was lifting Laura over the side.

"*Darling* José!" she burst out suddenly, and twined her
arms tightly round his neck.

At that Harry and Edward, who were already in the
boat, scrambled back on deck. They had forgotten to say
goodbye. And so each child said goodbye to each pirate,
kissing him and lavishing endearments on him.

"Go on! Go on!" muttered Jonsen impatiently.

Emily flung herself in his arms, sobbing as if her heart
would break.

"Don't make me go!" she begged: "Let me stay with you
always, always!" She clung tight to the lapels of his coat,
hiding her face in his chest: "Oh I *don't* want to go!"

Jonsen was strangely moved: for a moment, almost
toyed with the idea.

But the others were already in the boat.

"Come on!" said Otto, "or they'll go without you!"

"Wait! Wait!" shrieked Emily, and was over the side
and in the boat in a flash.

Jonsen shook his head confusedly. For this last time,
she had him puzzled.

But now, as they rowed across to the steamer, all the
children stood up in the boat, in danger of tumbling out,
and cried:

"Goodbye! Goodbye!"

"Adios!" cried the pirates, waving sentimental hands,
and guffawing secretly to each other.

"C-c-ome and see us in England!" came Edward's clear treble.

"Yes!" cried Emily: "Come and stay with us! All of you!—*Promise* you'll come and stay with us!"

"All right!" shouted Otto: "We'll come!"

"Come *soon!*"

"My babies!" wailed Rachel, "I've lost 'most all my babies!"

But now they were alongside the steamer: and soon they were mounting a rope ladder to her deck.

What a long way up it was! But at last they were all on board.

The little boat returned to the schooner.

The children never once looked after it.

And well might they forget it! For exciting as it had been to go onto a ship of any kind for the first time, to find themselves on this steamer was infinitely more so. The luxury of it! The white paint! The doors! The windows! The stairs! The brass!—A fairy palace, no: but a mundane wonder of a quite unimagined kind.

But they had little time now to take in the details. All the passengers, wild with curiosity, were gathered round them in a ring. As the dirty, disheveled little mites were handed one by one on board, a gasp went up. The story of the capture of the *Clorinda* by as fiendish a set of buccaneers as any in the past that roamed the same Caribbean was well known; and how the little innocents on board her had been taken and tortured to death before the eyes of the impotent captain. To see now face to face the victims of so foul a murder was for them, too, a thrill of the first water.

The tension was first broken by a beautiful young lady in a muslin dress. She sank on her knees beside little Harry, and folded him in her delicate arms.

"The little angel!" she murmured: "You poor little man, what horrors you have been through! How will you ever forget them?"

As if that were the signal, all the lady passengers fell on the astonished children and pitied them: while the men, less demonstrative, stood around with lumps in their throats.

Bewildered at first, it was not long before they rose to the occasion—as children generally will, when they find themselves the butt of indiscriminate adoration. Bless you, they were kings and queens! They were so sleepy they could hardly keep their eyes open: but they were not going to bed, not they! They had never been treated like this before. Heaven alone knew how long it would last. Best not waste a minute of it.

It was not long before they ceased even to be surprised, became convinced that it was all their right and due. They were very important people—quite unique.

Only Emily stood apart, shy, answering questions uncomfortably. She did not seem to be able to throw herself into her importance with the same zest as the others.

Even the passengers' children joined in the fuss and admiration: perhaps realising the opportunity which the excitement gave of avoiding their own bed-time. They began to bring (probably not without suggestion) their toys, as offerings to these new gods: and vied with each other in their generosity.

A shy little boy of about her own age, with brown eyes and a nice smile, his long hair brushed smooth as silk, his clothes neat and sweet-smelling, sidled up to Rachel.

"What's your name?" she asked him.

"Harold."

She told him hers.

"How much do you weigh?" he asked her.

"I don't know."

"You look rather heavy. May I see if I can lift you?"

"Yes."

He clasped his arms round her stomach from behind, leant back, and staggered a few paces with her. Then he set her down, the friendship cemented.

Emily stood apart; and for some reason, everyone unconsciously respected her reserve. But suddenly something seemed to snap in her heart. She flung herself facedownwards on the deck—not crying, but kicking convulsively. It was a huge great stewardess who picked her up and carried her, still quivering from head to foot, down to a neat, clean cabin. There, soothing and talking to her without ceasing, she undressed her, and washed her with warm water, and put her to bed.

Emily's head felt different to any way it had ever felt before: hardly as if it were her own. It sang, and went round like a wheel, without so much as with your leave or by your leave. But her body, on the other hand, was more than usually sensitive, absorbing the tender, smooth coolness of the sheets, the softness of the mattress, as a thirsty horse sucks up water. Her limbs drank in comfort at every pore: it seemed as if she could never be sated with it. She felt physical peace soaking slowly through to her marrow: and when at last it got there, her head became more quiet and orderly too.

All this while she had hardly heard what was said to her: only a refrain that ran through it all made any impression, *"Those wicked men . . . men . . . nothing but men . . . those cruel men. . . ."*

Men! It was perfectly true that for months and months she had seen nothing but men. To be at last back among other women was heavenly. When the kind stewardess bent over her to kiss her she caught tight hold of her, and buried her face in the warm, soft, yielding flesh, as if to sink herself in it. Lord, how unlike the firm, muscular bodies of Jonsen and Otto!

When the stewardess stood up again, Emily feasted her eyes on her, eyes grown large and warm and mysterious. The woman's enormous, swelling bosom fascinated her. Forlornly, she began to pinch her own thin little chest. Was it conceivable she would herself ever grow breasts like that—beautiful, mountainous breasts, that had to be cased in a sort of cornucopia? Or even firm little apples, like Margaret's?

Thank God she had not been born a boy! She was overtaken with a sudden revulsion against the whole sex of them. From the tips of her fingers to the tips of her toes she felt female: one with that exasperating, idiotic secret communion: initiate of the γυγαικεῖογ.

Suddenly Emily reached up and caught the stewardess by the head, pulling it down to her close: began whispering earnestly in her ear.

On the woman's face the first look of incredulity changed to utter stupefaction, from stupefaction to determination.

"My eye!" she said at last: "The cheek of the rascals! The impudence!"

Without another word she slipped out of the cabin. And you may imagine that the steamer captain, when he heard the trick that had been played upon him, was as astonished as she.

For a few moments after she had gone Emily lay staring at nothing, a very curious expression on her face indeed. Then, all of a sudden, she dropped asleep, breathing sweetly and easily.

But she only slept for about ten minutes; and when she

woke the cabin door was open, and in it stood Rachel and
her little boy friend.

"What do you want?" said Emily forbiddingly.

"Harold has brought his alligator," said Rachel.

Harold stepped forward, and laid the little creature on
Emily's coverlet. It was very small: only about six inches
long: a yearling: but an exact miniature of its adult self,
with the snub nose and round Socratic forehead that distinguish it from the crocodile. It moved jerkily, like a
clockwork toy. Harold picked it up by the tail: it spread
its paws in the air, and jerked from side to side, more like
clockwork than ever. Then he set it down again, and it
stood there, its tongueless mouth wide open and its harmless teeth looking like grains of sand-paper, alternately
barking and hissing. Harold let it snap at his finger—it
was plainly hungry, in the warmth down there. It darted
its head so fast you could hardly see it move: but its bite
was still so weak as to be painless, even to a child.

Emily drew a deep breath, fascinated.

"May I have him for the night?" she asked.

"All right," said Harold: and he and Rachel were summoned away by someone without.

Emily was translated into Heaven. So this was an alligator! She was actually going to sleep with an alligator!
She had thought that to anyone who had once been in an
earthquake nothing really exciting could happen again:
but then, she had not thought of this.

*There was once a girl called Emily, who slept with an
alligator . . .*

In search of greater warmth, the creature high-stepped
warily up the bed towards her face. About six inches away
it paused, and they looked each other in the eye, those
two children.

The eye of an alligator is large, protruding, and of a brilliant yellow, with a slit pupil like a cat's. A cat's eye, to the casual observer, is expressionless: though with attention one can distinguish in it many changes of emotion. But the eye of an alligator is infinitely more stony, and brilliant—reptilian.

What possible meaning could Emily find in such an eye? Yet she lay there, and stared, and stared: and the alligator stared too. If there had been an observer it might have given him a shiver to see them so—well, eye to eye like that.

Presently the beast opened his mouth and hissed again gently. Emily lifted a finger and began to rub the corner of his jaw. The hiss changed to a sound almost like a purr. A thin, filmy lid first covered his eye from the front backwards, then the outer lid closed up from below.

Suddenly he opened his eyes again, and snapped on her finger: then turned and wormed his way into the neck of her nightgown, and crawled down inside, cool and rough against her skin, till he found a place to rest. It is surprising that she could stand it, as she did, without flinching.

Alligators are utterly untamable.

4

From the deck of the schooner, Jonsen and Otto watched the children climb onto the steamer: watched their boat return, and the steamer get under way.

So: it had all gone without a hitch. No one had suspected his story—a story so simple as to be very nearly the truth.

They were gone.

Jonsen could feel the difference at once: and it seemed almost as if the schooner could. A schooner, after all, is a place for *men*. He stretched himself, and took a deep breath, feeling that a cloying, enervating influence was lifted. José was industriously sweeping up some of Rachel's abandoned babies. He swept them into the lee scuppers. He drew a bucket of water, and dashed it at them over the deck. The trap swung open—whew, it was gone, all that truck!

"Batten down that forehatch!" ordered Jonsen.

The men all seemed lighter of heart than they had been for many months: as if the weight they were relieved of had been enormous. They sang as they worked, and two friends playfully pummelled each other in passing—hard. The lean, masculine schooner shivered and plunged in the freshening evening breeze. A shower of spray for no particular reason suddenly burst over the bows, swept aft and dashed full in Jonsen's face. He shook his head like a wet dog, and grinned.

Rum appeared: and for the first time since the encounter with the Dutch steamer all the sailors got bestially drunk, and lay about the deck, and were sick in the scuppers. José was belching like a bassoon.

It was dark by then. The breeze dropped away again. The gaffs clanked aimlessly in the calm, with the motion of the sea: the empty sails flapped with reports like cannon, a hearty applause. Jonsen and Otto themselves remained sober, but they had not the heart to discipline the crew.

The steamer had long since disappeared into the dark. The foreboding which had oppressed Jonsen all the night before was gone. No intuition told him of Emily's whispering to the stewardess: of the steamer, shortly after,

meeting with a British gunboat: of the long series of lights
flickering between them. The gunboat, even now, was fast
overhauling him: but no premonition disturbed his short
peace.

He was tired—as tired as a sailor ever lets himself be.
The last twenty-four hours had been hard. He went below
as soon as his watch was over, and climbed into his bunk.

But he did not, at once, sleep. He lay for a while
conning over the step he had taken. It was really very
astute. He had returned the children, undoubtedly safe
and sound: Marpole would be altogether discredited.

Even to have landed them at Santa Lucia, his first intention, could never have closed the *Clorinda* episode so
completely, since the world at large would not have heard
of it: and it would have been difficult to produce them,
should need arise.

Indeed, it had seemed to be a choice of evils: either he
must carry them about always, as a proof that they were
alive, or he must land them and lose control of them. In
the first case, their presence would certainly connect him
with the *Clorinda* piracy, of which he might otherwise go
unsuspected: in the second, he might be convicted of
their murder if he could not produce them.

But this wonderful idea of his, now that he had carried
it out successfully, solved both difficulties.

It had been a near thing with that little bitch Margaret,
though . . . lucky the second boat had picked her up. . . .

The light from the cabin lamp shone into the bunk,
illuminating part of the wall defaced with Emily's puerile
drawings. As they caught his eye a frown gathered on his
forehead: but as well a sudden twinge affected his heart.
He remembered the way she had lain there, ill and helpless. He suddenly found himself remembering at least

forty things about her—an overwhelming flood of memories.

The pencil she had used was still among the bedding, and his fingers happened on it. There were still some white spaces not drawn on.

Jonsen could only draw two things: ships, and naked women. He could draw any type of ship he liked, down to the least detail—any particular ship he had sailed in, even. In the same way he could draw voluptuous, buxom women, also down to the least detail: in any position, and from any point of view: from the front, from the back, from the side, from above, from below: his foreshortening faultless. But set him to draw any third thing—even a woman with her clothes on—and he could not have produced a scribble that would have been recognisable.

He took the pencil: and before long there began to appear between Emily's crude uncertain lines round thighs, rounder bellies, high swelling bosoms, all somewhat in the manner of Rubens.

At the same time his mind was still occupied with reflections on his own astuteness. Yes, it had been a near thing with Margaret—it would have been awkward if, when he returned the party, there had been one missing.

A recollection descended on his mind like a cold shower, something he had completely forgotten about till then. His heart sank—as well it might:

"Hey!" he called to Otto on the deck above: "What was the name of that boy who broke his neck at Santa? Jim? Sam? What was he called?"

Otto did not answer, except by a long-drawn-out whistle.

CHAPTER TEN

Emily grew quite a lot during the passage to England on the steamer: suddenly shot up, as children will at that age. But she did it without any gawkiness: instead, an actual increase of grace. Her legs and arms, though longer, did not lose any of the nicety of their shape; and her grave face lost none of its attractiveness by being a fraction nearer your own. The only drawback was that she got pains in the calves of her legs now, and sometimes in her back: but those of course did not show. (They were all provided with clothes by a general collection, so it did not matter that she grew out of her old ones.)

She was a nice child: and being a little less shy than formerly was soon the most popular of all of them. Somehow, no one seemed to care very much for Margaret: old ladies used to shake their heads over her a good deal. At least, anyone could see that Emily had infinitely more sense.

You would never have believed that Edward after a few days washing and combing would look such a little gentleman.

After a short while Rachel threw Harold over, to be uninterrupted in her peculiar habits of parthenogenesis, eased now a little by the many presents of real dolls. But Harold became soon just as firm friends with Laura, young though she was.

Most of the steamer children had made friends with the seamen, and loved to follow them about at their romantic occupations—swabbing decks, and so on. One day, one of these men actually went a short way up the rigging (what little there was), leaving a glow of admiration on the deck below. But all this had no glamour for the Thorntons. Edward and Harry liked best to peer in at the engines: but what Emily liked best was to walk up and down the deck with her arm round the waist of Miss Dawson, the beautiful young lady with the muslin dresses: or stand behind her, while she did little watercolour compositions of toppling waves with wrecks foundering in them, or mounted dried tropical flowers in wreaths round photographs of her uncles and aunts. One day Miss Dawson took her down to her cabin and showed her all her clothes, every single item—it took hours. It was the opening of a new world to Emily.

The captain sent for Emily, and questioned her: but she added nothing to that first, crucial burst of confidence to the stewardess. She seemed struck dumb—with terror, or something: at least, he could get nothing out of her. So he wisely let her alone. She would probably tell her story in her own time: to her new friend, perhaps. But this she did not do. She would not talk about the schooner, or the pirates, or anything concerning them: what she wanted was to listen, to drink in all she could learn about England, where they were really going at last—that wonderfully exotic, romantic place.

Louisa Dawson was quite a wise young person for her

years. She saw that Emily did not want to talk about the
horrors she had been through: but considered it far better
that she should be made to talk than that she should
brood over them in secret. So when the days passed and
no confidences came she set herself to draw the child out.
She had, as everybody has, a pretty clear idea in her own
head of what life is like in a pirate vessel. That these little
innocents should have come through it alive was miraculous, like the three Hebrews in the fiery furnace.

"Where used you to live, when you were on the
schooner?" she asked Emily one day suddenly.

"Oh, in the hold," said Emily nonchalantly. "Is that
your Great-uncle *Vaughan,* did you say?"

In the hold. She might have known it. Chained, probably, down there in the darkness like blacks, with rats
running over them, fed on bread and water.

"Were you very frightened when there was a battle
going on? Did you hear them fighting over your head?"

Emily looked at her with her gentle stare: but kept
silence.

Louisa Dawson was very wise, in thus trying to ease the
load on the child's mind. But also she was consumed with
curiosity. It exasperated her that Emily would not talk.

There were two questions which she particularly
wanted to ask. One however seemed insuperably difficult
of approach. The other she could not contain:

"Listen, darling," she said, wrapping her arms around
Emily: "Did you ever actually see anyone killed?"

Emily stiffened palpably. "Oh no," she said: "Why
should we?"

"Didn't you ever even see a body?" she went on: "A
dead one?"

"No," said Emily. "There weren't any." She seemed to

meditate a while. "There weren't many," she corrected.

"You poor, poor little thing," said Miss Dawson, stroking her forehead.

But though Emily was slow to talk, Edward was not. Suggestion was hardly necessary. He soon saw what he was expected to say. It was also what he wanted to say. All those rehearsals with Harry, those springings into the main rigging, those stormings of the galley . . . they had seemed real enough at the time. Now he soon had no doubt about them at all. And Harry backed him up.

It was wonderful for Edward that everyone seemed ready to believe what he said. Those who came to him for tales of bloodshed were not sent empty away.

Nor did Rachel contradict him. The pirates were wicked—deadly wicked, as she had good reason to know. So they had probably done all Edward said: probably when she was not looking.

Miss Dawson did not always press Emily like this: she had too much sense. She spent a good deal of her time simply in tying more firmly the knots of the child's passion for her.

She was ready enough to tell her about England. But how strange it seemed that these humdrum narrations should interest anyone who had seen such romantic, terrible things as Emily had!

She told her all about London, where the traffic was so thick things could hardly pass, where things drove by all day, as if the supply of them would never come to an end. She tried also to describe trains, but Emily could not see them, somehow: all she could envisage was a steamer like this one, only going on land—but she knew that was not right.

What a wonderful person her Miss Dawson was! What

marvels she had seen. Emily had again the feeling she had
in the schooner's cabin: how time had slipped by, been
wasted. Now she would be eleven in a few months: a
great age: and in all that long life, how little of interest or
significance had happened to her! There were just two
things: her earthquake, of course, and she had slept with
an alligator: but what were these compared with the experiences of Miss Dawson, who knew London so well it
hardly seemed any longer wonderful to her, who could
not even count the number of times she had travelled in a
train?

Her Earthquake . . . it was a great possession. Dare she
tell Miss Dawson about it? Was it possible that it would
raise her a little in Miss Dawson's esteem, show that even
she, little Emily, had had experiences? But she never
dared. Suppose that to Miss Dawson earthquakes were as
familiar as railway trains: the fiasco would be unbearable.
As for the alligator, Miss Dawson had told Harold to take
it away, as if it was a worm.

Sometimes Miss Dawson sat silently fondling Emily,
looking now at her, now at the other children at play.
How difficult it was to imagine that these happy-looking
creatures had been, for months together, in hourly danger
of their lives! Why had they not died of fright? She was
sure that she would have. Or at least gone stark, staring,
raving mad?

She had always wondered how people survived even a
moment of danger without dropping dead with fear: but
months and months . . . and children. . . . Her head could
not swallow it.

As for that other question, how dearly she would have
liked to ask it, if only she could have devised a formula
delicate enough.

Meanwhile Emily's passion for her was nearing its crisis; and one day this was provoked. Miss Dawson kissed Emily three times, and told her in future to call her Lulu.

Emily jumped as if shot. Call this goddess by her Christian name? She burnt a glowing vermilion at the very thought. The Christian names of all grown-ups were sacred: something never to be uttered by childish lips: to do so, the most blasphemous disrespect.

For Miss Dawson to tell her to do so was as embarrassing as if she had seen written up in Church PLEASE SPIT.

Of course if Miss Dawson told her to call her Lulu, at least she must not call her Miss Dawson any more. But say . . . the Other Word aloud, her very lips refused.

And so for some time by elaborate subterfuges she managed to avoid calling her anything at all. But the difficulty of this increased in geometrical progression: it began to render all intercourse an intolerable strain.

Before long she was avoiding Miss Dawson.

Miss Dawson was terribly wounded: what could she have done to offend this strange child? ("Little Fairy-girl," she used to call her.) The darling had seemed so fond of her, but now . . .

So Miss Dawson used to follow her about the ship with hurt eyes, and Emily used to escape from her with scarlet cheeks. They had never had a real talk, heart to heart, again, by the time the steamer reached England.

2

When the steamer took in her pilot, you may imagine that her news travelled ashore; and also, that it quickly reached the *Times* newspaper.

Mr. and Mrs. Bas-Thornton, after the disaster, unable
to bear Jamaica any longer, had sold Ferndale for a song
and travelled straight back to England, where Mr. Thornton soon got posts as London dramatic critic to various
Colonial newspapers, and manipulated rather remote influence at the Admiralty in the hope of getting a punitive
expedition sent against the whole island of Cuba. It was
thus the *Times* which, in its quiet way, broke the news
to them, the very morning that the steamer docked at
Tilbury.

She was a long time doing it, owing to the fog, out of
which the gigantic noises of dockland reverberated unin-
telligibly. Voices shouted things from the quays. Bells
ting-a-linged. The children welded themselves into a
compact mass facing outwards, an improvised Argus determined to miss nothing whatever. But they could not
gather really what anything was about, much less everything.

Miss Dawson had taken charge of them all, meaning to
convey them to her aunt's London house till their relations could be found. So now she took them ashore, and
up to the train, into which they climbed.

"What are we getting into this box for?" asked Harry:
"Is it going to rain?"

It took Rachel several journeys up and down the steep
steps to get all her babies inside.

The fog, which had met them at the mouth of the river,
was growing thicker than ever. So they sat there in semi-
darkness at first, till a man came and lit the light. It was
not very comfortable, and horribly cold: but presently
another man came, and put in a big flat thing which was
hot: it was full of hot water, Miss Dawson said, and for
you to put your feet on.

Even now that she was in a train, Emily could hardly

believe it would ever start. She had become quite sure it was not going to when at last it did, jerking along like a shark would on a leash.

Then their powers of observation broke down. For the time they were full. So they played Up-Jenkins riotously all the way to London: and when they arrived hardly noticed it. They were quite loath to get out, and finally did so into as thick a pea-soup fog as London could produce at the tail end of the season. At this they began to wake up again, and jog themselves to remember that this really was *England,* so as not to miss things.

They had just realised that the train had run right inside a sort of enormous house, lit by haloed yellow lights and full of this extraordinary orange-coloured air, when Mrs. Thornton found them.

"Mother!" cried Emily. She had not known she could be so glad to see her. As for Mrs. Thornton, she was far beyond the bounds of hysteria. The little ones held back at first, but soon followed Emily's example, leaping on her and shouting: indeed it looked more like Actæon with his hounds than a mother with her children: their monkey-like little hands tore her clothes in pieces, but she didn't care a hoot. As for their father, he had totally forgotten how much he disliked emotional scenes.

"I slept with an alligator!" Emily was shouting at intervals: "Mother! I've slept with an alligator!"

Margaret stood in the background holding all their parcels. None of her relations had appeared at the station. Mrs. Thornton's eye at last took her in.

"Why, Margaret . . ." she began vaguely.

Margaret smiled and came forward to kiss her.

"Get out!" cried Emily fiercely, punching her in the chest. "She's *my* mother!"

"Get out!" shouted all the tothers. "She's *our* mother!"

Margaret fell back again into the shadows: and Mrs. Thornton was too distracted to be as shocked as she would normally have been.

Mr. Thornton however was just sane enough to take in the situation. "Come on, Margaret!" he said: "Margaret's *my* pal! Let's go and look for a cab!"

He took the girl's arm, bowing his fine shoulders, and walked off with her up the platform.

They found a cab, and brought it to the scene, and they all got in, Mrs. Thornton just remembering to say "How-d'you-do-good-bye" to Miss Dawson.

Packing themselves inside was difficult. It was in the middle of it all that Mrs. Thornton suddenly exclaimed:

"But where's John?"

The children fell immediately silent.

"Where is he?—Wasn't he on the train with you?"

"No," said Emily, and went as dumb as the rest.

Mrs. Thornton looked from one of them to another.

"John! Where is John?" she asked the world at large, a faint hint of uneasiness beginning to tinge her voice.

It was then that Miss Dawson showed a puzzled face at the window:

"*John?*" she asked: "Why, who is John?"

3

The children passed the spring at the house their father had taken in Hammersmith Terrace, on the borders of Chiswick: but Captain Jonsen, Otto, and the crew passed it in Newgate.

They were taken there as soon as the gunboat which apprehended them reached the Thames.

The children's bewilderment lasted. London was not

what they had expected, but it was even more astounding. From time to time however they would realise how this or that did chime in with something they had been told, though not at all with the idea that the telling had conjured up. On these occasions they felt something as Saint Matthew must have felt when, after recounting some trivial incident, he adds "That it might be fulfilled which was spoken by the Prophet So-and-so."

"Why look!" exclaimed Edward: "There's only toys in this store!"

"Why, don't you remember . . ." began Emily.

Yes, their mother had told them, on a visit to their father's general store in St. Anne's, that in London there were stores which not only sold toys but which sold toys only. At that time, they hardly knew what toys were. A cousin in England had once sent them out some expensive wax dolls, but even before the box was opened the wax had melted: consequently the only dolls they had were empty bottles, which they clothed with bits of rag. These had another advantage over the wax kind: you could feed them, poking it into the neck. If you put in some water too, in a day or so the food began to digest, visibly. The bottles with square shoulders they called He-beasties, and the bottles with round shoulders they called She-beasties.

Their other toys were mostly freakish sticks, and different kinds of seeds and berries. No wonder it seemed strange to them to imagine these things in a shop. But the idea engaged them, nevertheless. Down by the bathing-hole there were several enormous cotton-trees, which lift themselves on their roots right out of the earth, as if on stilts, making a big cage. One of these they dubbed their toy-shop: decorated it up with lace-bark, and strings of bright-coloured seeds and their other toys: then they would go inside and take turns to sell them to each other. So now this was the picture the phrase "toy-shop" evoked in them. No wonder the London kind was a surprise to them, seemed a very far-fetched fulfillment of the prophecy.

The houses in Hammersmith Terrace are tall, roomy, comfortable houses, though not big or aristocratic, with gardens running right down to the river.

It was a shock to them to find how dirty the river was. The litter-strewn mud when the tide was out somehow offended them much less than the sewery water when it was up. At low tide they would often climb down the wall and scrounge about in the mud for things of value to them happily enough. They stank like pole-cats when they came up again. Their father was sensible about dirt. He ordered a tub of water to be kept permanently outside the basement door, in which they must wash before entering the house: but none of the other children in the Terrace were allowed to play in the mud at all.

Emily did not play in the mud either; it was only the little ones.

Mr. Thornton was generally at a theatre till the small hours; and when he came home used to sit and write, and then he would go out, about dawn, to the post. The children were often awake in time to hear him going to bed. He drank whiskey while he worked, and that helped him to sleep all the morning (they had to be quiet too). But he got up for luncheon, and then he often had battles with their mother about the food. She would try to make him eat it.

All that spring they were an object of wonder to their acquaintances, as they had been on the steamer; and also an object of pity. In the wide world they had become

almost national figures: but it was easier to hide this from
them then than it would be nowadays. But people—
friends—would often come and tell them about the pirates: what wicked men they were, and how cruelly they
had maltreated them. Boys would generally ask to see
Emily's scar. These friends were especially sorry for
Rachel and Laura, who, as being the youngest, must have
suffered most. They used also to tell them about John's
heroism, and that he had died for his country just the
same as if he had grown up and become a real soldier:
that he had shown himself a true English gentleman, like
the knights of old were and the martyrs. They were to
grow up to be very proud of John, who though still a child
had dared to defy these villains and die rather than allow
anything to happen to his sisters.

The glorious deeds which Edward would occasionally
confess to were still received with an admiration hardly at
all tempered with incredulity. He had the intuition, by
now, to make them always done in defiance of Jonsen and
his crew, not, as formerly, in alliance with or superseding
them.

The children listened to all they were told: and according to their ages believed it. Having as yet little sense of
contradiction they blended it quite easily in their minds
with their own memories; or sometimes it even cast their
memories out. Who were they, children, to know better
what had happened to them than grown-ups?

Mrs. Thornton was a feeling, but an essentially Christian, woman. The death of John was a blow to her from
which she would never recover, as indeed the death of all
of them had once been. But she taught the children in
saying their prayers to thank God for John's noble end
and let it always be an example to them: and then she

taught them to ask God to forgive the pirates for all their cruelty to them. (She explained to them that God could only do this when they had been properly punished on Earth.) The only one who could not understand this at all was Laura—she was after all rather young. She used the same form of words as the others, yet contrived to imagine that she was praying to the pirates, not for them; so that it gradually came about that whenever God was mentioned in her hearing the face she imagined for Him was Captain Jonsen's.

Once more a phase of their lives was receding into the past, and crystallising into myth.

Emily was too old to say her prayers aloud, so no one could know whether she put in the same phrase as the others about the pirates or not. No one, in point of fact, knew much what Emily was thinking about anything, at that time.

4

One day a cab came for the whole family, and they drove together right into London. The cab took them into the Temple: and then they had to walk through twisting passages and up some stairs.

It was a day of full spring, and the large room into which they were ushered faced south. The windows were tall and heavily draped with curtains. After the gloomy stairs it seemed all sunshine and warmth. There was a big fire blazing, and the furniture was massive and comfortable, the dark carpet so thick it clung to their shoes.

A young man was standing in front of the fire when they came in. He was very correctly, indeed beautifully, dressed; and he was very handsome as well, like a prince. He smiled at them all pleasantly, and came forward and talked like an old friend. The suspicious eyes of the Liddlies soon accepted him as such. He gave their parents cake and wine: and then he insisted on the children being allowed a sip too, with some cake, which was very kind of him. The taste of the wine recalled to all of them that blowy night in Jamaica: they had had none since.

Soon some more people arrived. They were Margaret and Harry, with a small, yellow, fanatical-looking aunt. The two lots of children had not seen each other for a long time, so they only said hullo to each other very perfunctorily. Mr. Mathias, their host, was just as kind to the new arrivals.

Everyone was at great pains to make the visit appear a casual one; but the children all knew more or less that it was nothing of the sort, that something was presently going to happen. However, they could play-act too. Rachel presently climbed onto Mr. Mathias's knee. They all gathered round the fire, Emily sitting bolt upright on a foot-stool, Edward and Laura side by side in a capacious armchair.

In the middle of everyone talking there was a pause, and Mr. Thornton, turning to Emily, said: "Why don't you tell Mr. Mathias about your adventures?"

"Oh yes!" said Mr. Mathias. "Do tell me all about it. —Let me see, you're . . ."

"Emily," whispered Mr. Thornton.

"Age?"

"Ten."

Mr. Mathias reached for a piece of clean paper and a pen.

"What adventures?" asked Emily clearly.

"Well," said Mr. Mathias, "you started for England on a sailing-ship, didn't you? The *Clorinda?*"

"Yes. She was a barque."

, "And then what happened?"

She paused before answering.

"There was a monkey," she said judicially.

"A monkey?"

"And a lot of turtles," put in Rachel.

"Tell him about the pirates," prompted Mrs. Thornton.

Mr. Mathias frowned at her slightly. "Let her tell it in her own words, please."

"Oh yes," said Emily dully. "We were captured by pirates, of course."

Both Edward and Laura sat up at the word, stiff as spokes.

"Weren't you with them too, Miss Fernandez?" Mr. Mathias asked.

Miss Fernandez! Everyone turned to see who he could mean. He was looking at Margaret.

"Me?" she said suddenly, as if waking up.

"Yes, you! Go on!" said her aunt.

"Say yes," prompted Edward: "You were with us, weren't you?"

"Yes," said Margaret, smiling.

"Then why couldn't you say so?" hectored Edward.

Mr. Mathias silently noted this curious treatment of the eldest: and Mrs. Thornton told Edward he mustn't speak like that.

"Tell us what you remember about the capture, will you?" he asked, still of Margaret.

"The what?"

"Of how the pirates captured the *Clorinda.*"

She looked round nervously and laughed, but said nothing.

"The monkey was in the rigging, so they just came on the ship," Rachel volunteered.

"Did they—er—fight with the sailors? Did you see them hit anybody? Or threaten anybody?"

"Yes!" cried Edward, and jumped up from his chair, his eyes wide and inspired: "*Bing! Bang! Bong!*" he declared, thumping the seat at each word; then sat down again.

"They didn't," said Emily. "Don't be silly, Edward."

"Bing, bang, bong," he repeated, with less conviction.

"*Bung!*" contributed Harry to his support, from under the arm of the fanatical aunt.

"Bim-bam, bim-bam," sing-songed Laura, suddenly waking up and starting a tattoo of her own.

"Shut up!" cried Mr. Thornton. "Did you, or did you not, any of you, see them hit anybody?"

"Cut off their heads!" cried Edward. "And throw them in the sea!—Far, far . . ." his eyes became dreamy and sad.

"They didn't hit anybody," said Emily. "There wasn't anyone to hit."

"Then where were all the sailors?" asked Mr. Mathias.

"They were all up the rigging," said Emily.

"I see," said Mr. Mathias. "Er—didn't you say the monkey was in the rigging?"

"He broke his neck," said Rachel. She wrinkled up her nose disgustedly: "He was drunk."

"His tail was rotted," explained Harry.

"Well," said Mr. Mathias, "when they came on board, what did they do?"

There was a general silence.

"Come come! What did they do?—What did they do, Miss Fernandez?"

"*I* don't know."

"Emily?"

"I don't know."

He sat back in despair: "But you saw them!"

"No we didn't," said Emily. "We went in the deck-house."

"And stayed there?"

"We couldn't open the door."

"*Bang-bang-bang!*" Laura suddenly rapped out.

"Shut up!"

"And then, when they let you out?"

"We went on the schooner."

"Were you frightened?"

"What of?"

"Well: them."

"Who?"

"The pirates."

"Why should we?"

"They didn't do anything to frighten you?"

"To *frighten* us?"

"Coo! José did belch!" Edward interjected merrily, and began giving an imitation. Mrs. Thornton chid him.

"Now," said Mr. Mathias gravely, "there's something I want you to tell me, Emily. When you were with the pirates, did they ever do anything you didn't like? You know what I mean, something *nasty?*"

"Yes!" cried Rachel, and everyone turned to her. "He talked about drawers," she said in a shocked voice.

"What did he say?"

"He told us once not to toboggan down the deck on them," put in Emily uncomfortably.

"Was that all?"

"He shouldn't have talked about drawers," said Rachel.

"Don't *you* talk about them, then," cried Edward: "Smarty!"

"Miss Fernandez," said the lawyer diffidently, "have you anything to add to that?"

"What?"

"Well . . . what we are talking about."

She looked from one person to another, but said nothing.

"I don't want to press you for details," he said gently, "but did they ever—well, make suggestions to you?"

Emily fixed her glowing eyes on Margaret, catching hers.

"It's no good questioning Margaret," said the aunt morosely; "but it ought to be perfectly clear to you what has happened."

"Then I am afraid I must," said Mr. Mathias. "Another time, perhaps."

Mrs. Thornton had for some while been frowning and pursing her lips, to stop him.

"Another time would be much better," she said: and Mr. Mathias turned the examination back to the capture of the *Clorinda*.

But they seemed to have been strangely unobservant of what went on around them, he found.

5

When the others had all gone, Mathias offered Thornton, whom he liked, a cigar: and the two sat together for a while over the fire.

"Well," said Thornton, "did the interview go as you had expected?"

"Pretty much."

"I noticed you questioned them chiefly about the *Clorinda*. But you have got all the evidence you need on that score, surely?"

"Naturally I did. Anything they affirmed I could check exactly by Marpole's detailed affidavit. I wanted to test their reliability."

"And you found?"

"What I have always known. That I would rather extract information from the devil himself than from a child."

"But what information exactly do you need?"

"Everything. The whole story."

"You know it."

Mathias spoke with a hint of exasperation:

"Do you realise, Thornton, that without considerable help from them we may even fail to get a conviction?"

"What is the difficulty?" asked Thornton, in a peculiar, restrained tone.

"We could get a conviction for piracy of course. But since '37, piracy has ceased to be a hanging offence unless it is accompanied by murder."

"And is the killing of one small boy insufficient to count as murder?" asked Thornton, in the same cold voice.

Mathias looked at him curiously.

"We are able to guess at the probabilities of what happened," he said. "The boy was undoubtedly taken onto the schooner; and now he can't be found. But, strictly speaking, we have no proof that he is dead."

"He may, of course, have swum across the Gulf of Mexico and landed at New Orleans."

Thornton's cigar, as he finished speaking, snapped in two.

"I know this is . . ." began Mathias with professional

gentleness, then had the sense to check himself. "I am afraid there is no doubt which we can personally entertain that the lad is dead: but there is a legal doubt: and where there is legal doubt a jury might well refuse to convict."

"Unless they were carried away by an attack of common sense."

Mathias paused for a moment before asking:

"And the other children have dropped, as yet, no hint as to what precisely did happen to him?"

"None."

"Their mother has questioned them?"

"Exhaustively."

"Yet they must surely know."

"It is a great pity," said Thornton, deliberately, "that when the pirates decided to kill the child, they did not invite in his sisters to watch."

Mathias was ready to make allowances. He merely shifted his position and cleared his voice.

"Unless we can get definite evidence of murder, either of your boy or the Dutch captain, I am afraid there is a real danger of these men escaping with their lives: though they would of course be transported.—It's all highly unsatisfactory, Thornton," he went on confidentially. "We do not, as lawyers, like aiming at a conviction for piracy alone. It is too vague. The most eminent jurists have not even yet decided on a satisfactory definition of piracy. I doubt now if they ever will. One school holds that it is any felony committed on the high seas. But that definition does little except render the employment of a separate term otiose. Moreover, it is not accepted by other schools of thought."

"To the layman, at least, it would seem to be a queer

sort of piracy to commit suicide in one's cabin, or to perform an illegal operation on the captain's daughter."

"Well, you see the difficulties. Consequently we always prefer to make use of it simply as a make-weight with another more serious charge. Captain Kidd, for instance, was not, strictly speaking, hanged for piracy. The first count in his indictment, on which he was condemned, sets forth that he feloniously, intentionally, and with malice aforethought hit his own gunner on the head with a wooden bucket value eightpence. That is something definite. What *we* need is something definite. We have not got it. Take the second case, the piracy of the Dutch steamer. We are in the same difficulty there: a man is taken on board the schooner, he disappears. What happened? We can only surmise."

"Isn't there such a thing as turning King's Evidence?"

"Another most unsatisfactory proceeding, to which I should be very loath to have recourse. No, the natural and proper witnesses are the children. There is a kind of beauty in making them, who have suffered so much at the hands of these men, the instruments of justice upon them."

Mathias paused, and looked at Thornton narrowly.

"You haven't been able, in all these weeks, to get the smallest hint from them with regard to the death of Captain Vandervoort either?"

"None."

"Well, is it your impression that they do truly know nothing, or that they have been terrorised into hiding something?"

Thornton gave a gentle sigh, almost of relief.

"No," he said, "I don't think they have been terrorised. But I do think they may know something they won't tell."

"But, why?"

"Because during the time they were on the schooner they plainly got very fond of this man Jonsen, and of his lieutenant, the man called Otto."

Mathias was incredulous.

"Is it possible for children to be mistaken in a man's whole nature like that?"

The look of irony on Thornton's face attained an intensity that was almost diabolical.

"I think it is possible," he said, "even for children to make such a mistake."

"But this . . . affection: it is highly improbable."

"It is a fact."

Mathias shrugged. After all, a criminal lawyer is not concerned with facts, he is concerned with probabilities. It is the novelist who is concerned with facts, whose job it is to say what a particular man did do on a particular occasion: the lawyer does not, cannot be expected to go further than to show what the ordinary man would be most likely to do under presumed circumstances.

Mathias, as he conned these paradoxes, smiled a little grimly. It would never do to give utterance to them.

"I think if they know anything I shall be able to find it out," was all he said.

"D'you mean to put them in the box?" Thornton asked suddenly.

"Not all of them, certainly: Heaven forbid! But we shall have to produce one of them at least, I am afraid."

"Which?"

"Well. We had intended it to be the Fernandez girl. But she seems . . . unsatisfactory?"

"Exactly." Then Thornton added with a characteristic forward jerk, "She was sane enough when she left Jamaica.

—Though always a bit of a fool."

"Her aunt tells me she seems to have lost her memory: or a great part of it. No, if I call her it will simply be to exhibit her condition."

"Then?"

"I think I will call your Emily."

Thornton stood up.

"Well," he said, "you'll have to settle with her yourself what she's to say. Write it out, and make her learn it by heart."

"Certainly," said Mathias, looking at his finger-nails. "I am not in the habit of going into court unprepared.—It's bad enough having a child in the box anyway," he went on.

Thornton paused at the door.

"—You can never count on them. They say what they think you want them to say. And then they say what they think the opposing counsel wants them to say too—if they like his face."

Thornton gesticulated—a foreign habit.

"I think I'll take her to Madame Tussaud's on Thursday afternoon and try my luck," ended Mathias: and the two bade each other goodbye.

6

Emily enjoyed the wax-works; even though she did not know that a wax-work of Captain Jonsen, his scowling face bloody and a knife in his hand, was already in contemplation. She got on well with Mr. Mathias. She felt very grown-up, going out at last without the little ones endlessly tagging. Afterwards he took her to a bun-shop in Baker Street, and tried to persuade her to pour out his tea

for him: but she turned shy at that, and he had in the end
to do it for himself.

Mr. Mathias, like Miss Dawson, spent a good deal of his
time and energy in courting the child's liking. He was at
least sufficiently successful for it to come as a complete
surprise to her, when he presently began to throw out
questions about the death of Captain Vandervoort. Their
studied casualness did not deceive her for a moment. He
learnt nothing: but she was hardly home, and his carriage
departed, than she was violently sick. Presumably she had
eaten too many cream buns. But, as she lay in bed sipping
from a tumbler of water in that mood of fatalism which
follows on the heels of vomiting, Emily had a lot to think
over, as well as an opportunity of doing so without
emotion.

Her father was spending a rare evening at home: and
now he stood unseen in the shadows of her bedroom,
watching her. To his fantastic mind, the little chit seemed
the stage of a great tragedy: and while his bowels of
compassion yearned towards the child of his loins, his
intellect was delighted at the beautiful, the subtle com-
bination of the contending forces which he read into the
situation. He was like a powerless stalled audience, which
pities unbearably, but would not on any account have
missed the play.

But as he stood now watching her, his sensitive eyes
communicated to him an emotion which was not pity and
was not delight: he realised, with a sudden painful shock,
that he was afraid of her!

But surely it was some trick of the candlelight, or of her
indisposition, that gave her face momentarily that inhuman, stony, basilisk look?

Just as he was tiptoeing from the room, she burst out

into a sudden, despairing moan, and leaning half out of her bed began again an ineffectual, painful retching. Thornton persuaded her to drink off her tumbler of water, and then held her hot moist temples between his hands till at last she sank back, exhausted, in a complete passivity, and slipped off to sleep.

There were several other occasions after this when Mr. Mathias took her out on excursions, or simply came and examined her at the house. But still he learnt nothing.

What was in her mind now? I can no longer read Emily's deeper thoughts, or handle their cords. Henceforth we must be content to surmise.

As for Mathias, there was nothing for it but to accept the defeat at her hands, and then explain it away to himself. He ceased to believe that she had anything to hide, because, if she had, he was convinced she could not have hidden it.

But if she could not give him any information, she remained, spectacularly speaking, a most valuable witness. So, as Thornton had suggested, he set his clerk to copy out in his beautiful hand a sort of Shorter Catechism: and this he gave to Emily and told her to learn it.

She took it home and showed it to her mother, who said Mr. Mathias was quite right, she was to learn it. So Emily pinned it to her looking-glass, and learnt the answers to two new questions every morning. Her mother would hear her these with her other lessons, and badgered her a lot for the singsong way she repeated them. But how can one speak naturally anything learnt by heart, Emily wondered? It is impossible. And Emily knew this catechism backwards and forwards, inside and out, before the day came.

Once more they drove into town: but this time it was to the Central Criminal Court. The crowd outside was enormous, and Emily was bundled in with the greatest rapidity. The building was impressive, and full of policemen, and the longer she had to wait in the little room where they were shown the more nervous she became. Would she remember her piece, or would she forget it? From time to time echoing voices sounded down the corridors, summoning this person or that. Her mother stayed with her, but her father only looked in occasionally, when he would give some news to her mother in a low tone. Emily had her catechism with her, and read it over and over.

Finally a policeman came, and conducted them into the court.

A criminal court is a very curious place. The seat of a ritual quite as elaborate as any religious one, it lacks in itself any impressiveness or symbolism of architecture. A robed judge in court looks like a Catholic bishop would, if he were to celebrate mass in some municipal bath-house. There is nothing to make one aware that here the Real Presence is: the presence of death.

As Emily came into court, past the many men in black gowns writing with their quill pens, she did not at first see judge, jury, or prisoners. Her eye was caught by the face of the clerk, where he sat below the bench. It was an old and very beautiful face, cultured, unearthly refined. His head laid back, his mouth slightly open, his eyes closed, he was gently sleeping.

That face remained etched on her mind as she was shown her way into the box. Then the oath, which formed the opening passages of her catechism, was administered; and with its familiar phrases her nervousness vanished, and with complete confidence she sang out her responses to the familiar questions which Mr. Mathias, in fancy dress, was putting to her. But until he had finished she kept her eyes fixed on the rail in front of her, for fear something should confuse her. At last, however, Mr. Mathias sat down; and Emily began to look around her. High above the sleeping man sat another, with a face even more refined, but wide awake. His voice, when now he spoke a few words to her, was the kindest she had ever heard. Dressed in his strange disguise, toying with a pretty nosegay, he looked like some benign old wizard who spent his magic in doing good.

Beneath her was the table where so many other wigged men were sitting. One was drawing funny faces: but his own was grave. Two more were whispering together.

Now another man was on his feet. He was shorter than Mr. Mathias, and older, and in no way good-looking or even interesting. He in turn began to ask her questions.

He, Watkin, the defending counsel, was no fool. He had not failed to notice that, among all the questions Mathias had put to her, there had been no reference to the death of Captain Vandervoort. That could only mean either that the child knew nothing of it, itself a valuable lacuna in the evidence to establish, or that what she did know was somehow in his clients' favour. Up till now, he had meant to pursue the obvious tactics—question her on the evidence she had already given, perhaps frighten her, at any rate confuse her and make her contradict herself. But anyone, even a jury, could see through that. Nor was there any hope, under any circumstances, of a total acquittal: the most he could hope for was escape from the murder charge.

He suddenly decided to change his whole policy. When

he spoke, his voice too was kind (though it lacked per-
force the full benign timbre of the judge's). He would
make no attempt to confuse her. By his sympathy with
her, he hoped for the sympathy, himself, of the court.

His first few questions were of a general nature: and he
continued them until her answers were given with complete confidence.

"Now, my dear young lady," he said at last, "there is
just one more question I want to ask you: and please answer it loudly and clearly, so that we can all hear. We
have been told about the Dutch steamer, which had the
animals on board. Now a very horrible thing has been
suggested." His voice grew blandly incredulous:—"It has
been said that a man was taken off the steamer, the captain of it in fact, onto the schooner, and that he was murdered there. Now what I want to ask you is this. Did you
see any such thing happen?"

Those who were watching the self-contained Emily saw
her turn very white, and begin to tremble. Suddenly she
gave a shriek: then after a second's pause she began to
sob. Everyone listened in an icy stillness, their hearts in
their mouths. Through her tears they heard, they all
heard, the words: ". . . He was all lying in his blood . . . he
was awful! He . . . he died, he said something and then he
died!"

That was all that was articulate. Watkin sat down,
thunderstruck. The effect on the court could hardly have
been greater. As for Mathias, he did not show surprise: he
looked more like a man who has digged a pit into which
his enemy has fallen.

The judge leant forward and tried to question her: but
she only sobbed and screamed. He tried to soothe her: but
by now she had become too hysterical for that. She had

already, however, said quite enough for the matter in
hand: and they let her father come forward and lift her
out of the box.)

As he stepped down with her she caught sight for the
first time of Jonsen and the crew, huddled up together in a
sort of pen. But they were much thinner than the last time
she had seen them. The terrible look on Jonsen's face as
his eye met hers, what was it that it reminded her of?

Her father hurried her home. As soon as she was in the
cab she became herself again with a surprising rapidity.
She began to talk about all she had seen, just as if it had
been a party: the man asleep, and the man drawing funny
faces, and the man with the bunch of flowers, and had she
said her piece properly?

"Captain was there," she said: "Did you see him?"

"What was it all about?" she asked presently: "Why did
I have to learn all those questions?"

Mr. Thornton made no attempt to answer her questions: he even shrank back, physically, from touching his
child Emily. His mind reeled with the many possibilities.
Was it conceivable she was such an idiot as really not to
know what it was all about? Could she possibly not know
what she had done? He stole a look at her innocent little
face, even the tear-stains now gone. What was he to
think?

But as if she read his thoughts, he saw a faint cloud
gather.

"What are they going to do to Captain?" she asked, a
faint hint of anxiety in her voice.

Still he made no answer. In Emily's head the captain's
face, as she had last seen it . . . what was it she was trying
to remember?

Suddenly she burst out:

"Father, *what* did happen to Tabby in the end, that dreadful windy night in Jamaica?"

7

Trials are quickly over, once they begin. It was no time before the judge had condemned these prisoners to death and was trying someone else with the same concentrated, benevolent, individual attention.

Afterwards, a few of the crew were reprieved and transported.

The night before the execution, Jonsen managed to cut his throat: but they found out in time to bandage him up. He was unconscious by the morning, and had to be carried to the gallows in a chair: indeed, he was finally hanged in it. Otto bent over once and kissed his forehead; but he was completely insensible.

It was the Negro cook, however, according to the account in the *Times*, who figured most prominently. He showed no fear of death himself, and tried to comfort the others.

"We have all come here to die," he said: *"That"* (pointing to the gallows) "was not built for nothing. We shall certainly end our lives in this place: nothing can now save us. But in a few years we should die in any case. In a few years the judge who condemned us, all men now living, will be dead. *You* know that I die innocent: anything I have done I was forced to do by the rest of you. But I am not sorry. I would rather die now, innocent, than in a few years perhaps guilty of some great crime."

8

It was a few days later that the term began, and Mr. and
Mrs. Thornton took Emily to her new school at Black-
heath. While they remained to tea with the head mistress,
Emily was introduced to her new playmates.

"Poor little thing," said the mistress, "I hope she will
soon forget the terrible things she has been through. I
think our girls will have an especially kind corner in their
hearts for her."

In another room, Emily with the other new girls was
making friends with the older pupils. Looking at that gentle, happy throng of clean innocent faces and soft graceful
limbs, listening to the ceaseless, artless babble of chatter
rising, perhaps God could have picked out from among
them which was Emily: but I am sure that I could not.

ABOUT THE AUTHOR

RICHARD HUGHES was born in England in 1900, attended Charterhouse School and served in the British Army before going to Oxford. While still an undergraduate, he was on the contributing staffs of two London weeklies, had a play produced in London and published a book of poems.

In 1922 he left Oxford, spending some time in Central Europe before going back to Wales and a period of writing— poems, stories and three more plays. After his second visit to the United States, he returned to found a Welsh dramatic company. At twenty-four he had had three plays staged in London.

After a trip to Ireland as a deck hand on a small sailing vessel in 1925, he retired to an Adriatic island, where he began writing *A High Wind in Jamaica*—a book he finished three years later in Connecticut. Its first publication was in the U.S. under the title *The Innocent Voyage*, establishing his reputation as an outstanding novelist. A book of children's stories, *The Spider's Palace*, followed. His second novel, *In Hazard*, was published in 1938, and another volume of children's stories, *Don't Blame Me*, a year later. *The Fox in the Attic*, published in 1961, was widely praised and was a best seller.

During World War II Mr. Hughes worked as a civilian for the Admiralty, and later collaborated on its official history. For three years he lectured periodically in London as Gresham Professor in Rhetoric.

Since 1946, Mr. Hughes, his wife and five children have lived in North Wales. All his life, however, he has "felt from time to time an impelling need to travel—whether dabbling in Balkan revolutions, shooting the Canadian Rapids with Indian trappers, or bluffing my way unarmed among the Berber tribesmen in Southern Morocco."